W9-BFA-050

For current pricing information,
or to learn more about this or any Nextext title,
call us toll-free at **1-800-323-5435**
or visit our web site at www.nextext.com.

STORIES IN HISTORY

REFORMATION AND ENLIGHTENMENT

1500–1800

Cover illustration: Todd Leonardo

Printed in the United States of America

ISBN 0-618-14223-1

4 5 6 7 8 9 — QVK— 06 05 04

Table of Contents

BACKGROUND

The Reformation 11
Religious Warfare 13
The Enlightenment 17
Political Revolution 20
Scientific Revolution 24
Time Line 26

PART I: RELIGION AND RELIGIOUS WARS

1521
The Trial of Martin Luther 28
by Lynnette Brent

*Luther was a law student who had a powerful
religious experience during a thunderstorm. He
became a priest and tried to reform the Church.
This is his story.*

1556
From Soldier to Saint 40
by Walter Hazen

*Ignatius Loyola gave up being a soldier for
Spain and became a "soldier of Christ." He
formed a unique religious group, the Jesuits, that
had a major role in the Catholic Reformation.*

1585–1642

Cardinal Richelieu 49

by Barbara Littman

*Some people said he used lies and trickery to
reach his goals. But this chief minister of France
would do anything to unify his Catholic country
and break Hapsburg control of Europe—even
ally himself with Protestants!*

1688

The Glorious Revolution 61

by Judy Volem

*The Glorious Revolution was a revolution in
which no blood was shed. There had, however,
been way too much bloodshed earlier. The brutal
George Jeffreys, Lord Chief Justice of England,
was responsible for a lot of it. This is the story of
his reign of terror.*

PART II: THE ENLIGHTENMENT

c. 1600–1778

Man and Society: Four Views 72

by Judith Lloyd Yero

*In this imaginary debate between four
Enlightenment thinkers, the ideas of
Thomas Hobbes, John Locke, the Baron
Charles de Montesquieu, and Jean-Jacques
Rousseau are explained.*

c. 1718–1778

Voltaire and Frederick the Great 82

by Marianne McComb

*The French philosopher Voltaire laughed at
the rich and powerful in his writing, yet King
Frederick the Great invited Voltaire to his court.
They got along very well for three years. Finally,
they got on each other's nerves—and Voltaire
ended up spending time in jail!*

1750

At the Salon of Madame Geoffrin 92

by Stephen Feinstein

*Marie-Thérèse Geoffrin was a wealthy French
woman who loved to have philosophers, writers,
artists, scientists, and other exciting thinkers come
to her house to share ideas. These gatherings
were called salons. Attend one of her salons, and
see what people are wearing, eating, and saying.*

1762–1796

Catherine the Great 100

by Carole Pope

*When she was 15, Catherine left Germany
to marry the heir to the Russian throne.
Unfortunately, Peter III was not in his right
mind. This is the story of how Catherine became
one of Russia's greatest rulers.*

1760–1772
Thomas Jefferson 110
by Lynnette Brent

*The man who wrote America's Declaration
of Independence was deeply influenced by
Enlightenment thinkers. This story focuses
on his days as a young law student and an
observer of the American political scene.*

1789
"Let Them Eat Cake" 119
by Walter Hazen

*France's government was deeply in debt.
The peasants in the countryside were starving.
When Queen Marie Antoinette was told they
had no bread, she is supposed to have said,
"Why, let them eat cake." The people of Paris
rebelled, starting a revolution. In the process,
they beheaded Louis XVI and the queen.*

1791–1803
Toussaint L'Ouverture 131
by Barbara Littman

*In the 1780s, encouraged by the American
Revolution, there were a number of colonial
uprisings in the Americas, but only one
succeeded. In 1791 in Haiti, Toussaint
L'Ouverture, a freed black slave, helped
to lead a rebellion against the French.*

1492–c. 1650

**Tomatoes Are Poison and Potatoes
Cause Leprosy**...148
by Dee Masters

As Europeans moved into the newly explored
parts of the world, they brought plants, animals,
and diseases with them. When ships traveled
back to Europe from the colonies in the Western
Hemisphere, they carried new foods and plants
to Europe. Lives on both sides of the Atlantic
changed forever.

1609–1642

"And Yet, It Does Move!"...................................159
by Judith Lloyd Yero

Galileo took a new approach to science. Instead
of following traditional teachings of the Church,
he looked at nature directly and made new
discoveries. When Galileo argued that the Earth
revolves around the sun, the Catholic Church put
him before the Inquisition. Under pressure,
Galileo took back what he had said. But his
ideas soon spread throughout Europe.

1721
Lady Mary's Advice 170
by Stephen Feinstein

Lady Mary Montagu noticed that women in
Turkey protected their children against smallpox
with liquid taken from the sores of people who
had the disease. As smallpox sweeps through
London, Lady Mary gives some controversial
advice to a worried mother.

Sources 181

Glossary 185

Acknowledgements 191

About this Book

The stories are historical fiction. They are based on historical fact, but some of the characters and events may be fictional. In the Sources section, you'll learn which is which and where the information came from.

The illustrations are all historical. If they are from a time different from the story, the caption tells you. Original documents and quotes from historic people appear throughout the book. Maps let you know where things were.

Items explained in People and Terms to Know are repeated in the Glossary. Look there if you come across a name or term you don't know.

Historians do not always agree on the exact dates of events in the past. The letter c before a date means "about" (from the Latin word circa).

If you would like to read more about these exciting times, you will find recommendations in Reading on Your Own.

Background

I disapprove of what you say, but I will defend to the death your right to say it.

—Voltaire

▲ The French philosopher Voltaire raises his arm to make a point during a dinner with other thinkers.

The Reformation

Here I stand, I cannot do otherwise.

—Martin Luther, at the Diet of Worms

The Reformation began as people tried to reform the Catholic Church, but politics got in the way. Strong kings and princes were competing with each other. New Protestant churches denied the power of the pope and tried to approach God in new, more direct ways. Northern European rulers protected their Protestant leaders. In response to Protestantism, the Catholic Church began a Reformation of its own.

The Rise of Protestantism

In 1517, a German priest named Martin Luther made a list of arguments against some practices in the Church. He nailed the list to the door of a church in Wittenberg. Luther's act started the Protestant Reformation.

Luther taught that people could win salvation only by faith in God's gift of forgiveness. He attacked the authority of the pope. Luther said that all Church teachings should be clearly based on the Bible and that people did not need priests to interpret the Bible for them. Though Holy Roman Emperor Charles V condemned Luther at the Diet (or assembly) of Worms in 1521, his ideas spread through Germany and beyond.

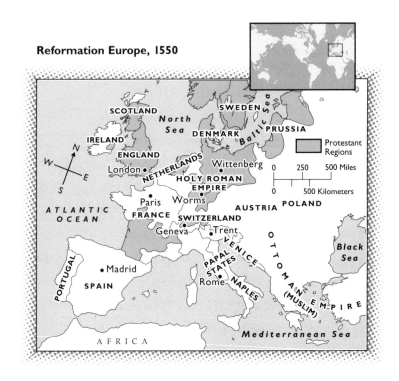

Reformation Europe, 1550

All over Europe, Protestant churches were formed. In Switzerland and the German states of the Holy Roman Empire, Ulrich Zwingli and John Calvin drew many followers. In France, Calvin's followers fought for religious freedom. In Scotland, John Knox won many converts. In England, King Henry VIII set up the Church of England.

Catholic Reformation

In response to Protestantism, the Catholic Church tried to reform itself. This movement was called the Catholic Reformation. The Church took several

important steps. The pope called a major confer-
ence of Church leaders, the Council of Trent
(1545–1563), which banned some bad practices. The
Church also approved several new religious groups
that stressed holiness and a simple way of life. The
most important was The Society of Jesus, or Jesuits,
founded by Ignatius Loyola in 1534.

Religious Warfare

*War is one of the scourges with which it has
pleased God to afflict men.*

—Cardinal Richelieu

Some parts of Europe remained solidly Catholic,
such as Spain, Portugal, and present-day Italy.
Others became Protestant, such as England,
Denmark, and Sweden. Some areas were strongly
divided. France, for example, had a large Protestant
minority. The Holy Roman Empire, which included
present-day Germany and much of Central Europe,
was also divided between Protestants and Catholics.
In the 1540s, a century of religious warfare began all
over Europe. The final part of this period was the
Thirty Years' War.

The Thirty Years' War

The Thirty Years' War actually was a series of wars that were fought between 1618 and 1648. It began with a civil war in Bohemia (see map on page 55), a small country in Central Europe, but the conflict soon spread. Before it was over, much of Central Europe was in ruins.

Attacks by soldiers on villagers were common events during the Thirty Years' War. ▶

The Thirty Years' War was partly religious and partly political. When the war began, the Hapsburgs, a Catholic ruling family, controlled Austria and the Holy Roman Empire. The Hapsburgs wanted to control all of Europe and wipe out Protestantism. Opposing them was France, whose government was headed by Cardinal Richelieu. Although France was Catholic, Richelieu wanted to reduce the power of the Hapsburgs. He joined Protestant Germany, Sweden, and Denmark. Together, they broke the Hapsburgs' control of Europe.

Religious Conflict in England

In England, the government was divided. The king, Charles I, offended Protestants by marrying a Catholic. Parliament, the main governing body, included many Puritans, Protestants who wanted to reform the Church of England. In 1642, problems between the king and Parliament led to a civil war. The war began because Charles I shut down Parliament and took away the Protestants' freedoms. Finally, a Puritan leader, Oliver Cromwell, led an army against Charles. By 1648, the Puritans had won. In January 1649, Charles was tried for treason, sentenced to death, and beheaded. Cromwell became England's ruler.

▲

The climax of the English Civil War was the execution
of King Charles I by his Puritan enemies.

Charles's son, Charles II, fled to France. After a
while, the English people grew tired of Cromwell's
strict rule. When Cromwell died in 1658, the
English people wanted Charles II to return. In 1660,
Charles II was made England's ruler. This event
was called the Restoration.

In 1685, Charles II died, and his brother, James II,
became king. James tried to change the country back
to Catholicism. He used his power against the English
people in terrible ways. Finally, even his own troops
were against him. In 1688, James fled to France. Then
Protestant leaders invited James's daughter Mary and
her Protestant husband, William of Orange, to become
the new queen and king. This event is called the
Glorious Revolution because no blood was shed.

The Enlightenment

Man is born free, and everywhere he is in chains.
—Jean Jacques Rousseau

From the late 1600s to the late 1700s, a group of philosophers had a great influence on political events. These thinkers were part of a movement called the Enlightenment. Most Enlightenment thinkers supported human rights and religious and political freedom. Because the Enlightenment challenged long-standing authorities such as kings, it encouraged the American and French Revolutions. The Enlightenment also influenced European rulers to make reforms in their countries. Among these reforming rulers were Frederick II of Prussia and Catherine the Great of Russia.

◀ This image comes from the title page of Thomas Hobbes's book *Leviathan*. The huge figure made up of tiny people shows Hobbes's view that everyone in a state must give up individual rights to the government.

Major Thinkers of the Enlightenment

Thinker	Idea
Thomas Hobbes English 1588–1679	*social contract* People are joined to their government by a contract. They agree to give up some rights in return for law and order.
John Locke English 1632–1704	*natural rights* People have rights to life, liberty, and property.
Baron Charles de Montesquieu French 1689–1755	*separation of powers* Divisions of government should control each other.
Voltaire French 1694–1778	*religious freedom* People should not be punished for their beliefs.
Jean-Jacques Rousseau French 1712–1778	*natural goodness* People in their "natural state" are good; civilization makes them slaves.

Thinker	Effect
Hobbes	Hobbes's ideas supported absolute rulers.
Locke	Locke's ideas influenced the American Declaration of Independence.
Montesquieu	Montesquieu's ideas shaped new governments in the United States, France, and Latin America.
Voltaire	Voltaire's ideas influenced enlightened European rulers and the American and the French bills of rights.
Rousseau	Rousseau's ideas inspired the leaders of the French Revolution.

Political Revolution

We hold these truths to be self-evident: that all
men are created equal. . . .

—The Declaration of Independence

In the 1760s, groups of well-educated political leaders in the Americas and France began to be influenced by the ideas of the Enlightenment. These leaders wanted to organize new societies that were based on human freedom rather than the rule of kings.

American Revolution

In the mid-1760s, England tightened its hold over its thirteen American colonies. The colonists were angered by the new taxes and other laws. They began a series of protests. As the years passed, relations between England and the colonies grew worse. In April 1775, fighting broke out between colonists and English troops. The American Revolution had begun.

In July 1776, the colonies issued the Declaration of Independence, which established their new nation, the United States of America. Written by Thomas Jefferson, it was based on the ideas of the

Enlightenment. The Revolutionary War between England and the United States lasted until the American victory in 1783. In 1787, leaders of the new nation drafted a constitution. The form of government they created came in part from Enlightenment ideas. When a Bill of Rights was added to the Constitution in 1791, it also showed the influence of the Enlightenment.

▲
A cartoon from the time of the American Revolution shows King George III of England being thrown by "the Horse America."

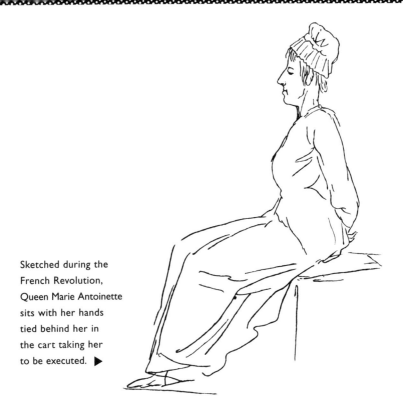

Sketched during the French Revolution, Queen Marie Antoinette sits with her hands tied behind her in the cart taking her to be executed. ▶

French Revolution

In France, the American Revolution stirred a powerful response. The Americans had put the ideas of Enlightenment thinkers into practice. But in France, the Church, the nobles, and the king still ruled society. These groups were wealthy and satisfied. They ignored the starving peasants and the rising middle class, who suffered under heavy taxes.

In 1789, King Louis XVI ran out of money and called France's legislature together to vote him more taxes. The common people surprised him by demanding more voting power and a written constitution. They formed a National Assembly and forced Louis to approve it. Over the next several years, this Assembly passed many reforms and set up a new constitution. It ended privileges and gave France freedom of the press and religion, individual rights, and rights of assembly. Meanwhile, however, the revolution took a more violent turn. On July 14, 1789, an angry mob stormed the Bastille, a famous prison in Paris. In June 1791, the royal family attempted to flee France but was captured near the border and returned to Paris under guard. During 1793 and 1794, the "Reign of Terror" gripped France. Revolutionary leaders beheaded thousands of people. Among them were King Louis XVI and Queen Marie Antoinette.

Revolution in Haiti

The French Revolution helped spread Enlightenment ideas. In the French colony of Haiti in the Caribbean Sea, a slave revolt began in 1791. It was led by Toussaint L'Ouverture (too•SAN loo•vehr•TYOOR), a former slave. He was captured by the French and died in prison, but his revolution succeeded. In 1804, Haiti became the first Latin American country to achieve independence.

▲
The items in this room at the French Royal Academy of Sciences show a wide range of scientific research.

Scientific Revolution

In the mid 1500s, European scientists began to look at nature in a new way. This is called the Scientific Revolution. Instead of following Church teachings about nature, scientists observed nature for themselves. They learned by doing experiments and drawing conclusions. This led to many advances in science and to the scientific method used today.

The revolution began when astronomers such as Nicolaus Copernicus, Tycho Brahe (BRAH•hee), and Galileo Galilei (GAL•uh•LEE•oh GAL•uh•LAY) watched the skies and published new ideas about the universe. Other scientists followed with new discoveries. William Harvey described the human heart and the movement of the blood. Johannes Kepler defined how planets move. Sir Isaac Newton discovered the law of gravity. Robert Boyle pioneered the study of chemistry. And Sir Francis Bacon and René Descartes produced works that outlined the new scientific method.

The Columbian Exchange

After the voyages of Christopher Columbus in the 1490s, the lands and peoples of the Americas became linked to Europe. As ships sailed between Europe and the New World, new plants, animals, and diseases traveled with them. This is today called the Columbian Exchange. (The name *Columbian* refers to Columbus.)

Ships from the Americas brought new plants to Europe. These included tomatoes, squash, pineapples, tobacco, and cacao beans (for chocolate). Corn and potatoes from the New World became very important. They enriched European diets and helped to increase the population.

Ships from Europe brought horses, cattle, and pigs to the Americas. New foods included bananas, black-eyed peas, and yams. But Europeans also brought such new diseases as smallpox and measles to native peoples in the Americas, causing millions of deaths.

Time Line

1492—Columbus reaches the Americas, beginning the process of the Columbian Exchange.

1517—Martin Luther states his beliefs.

1521—Luther is condemned at the Diet of Worms.

1534—Ignatius Loyola founds the Society of Jesus.

1543—Copernicus publishes his ideas about the sun and planets.

1545–1563—The Council of Trent meets.

1618–1648—The Thirty Years' War is fought.

1633—Galileo is tried by the Church for his beliefs.

1642—English Civil War begins.

1649—Charles I is executed.

1660—Charles II is restored as king of England.

1688—James II is overthrown in the Glorious Revolution.

1740—Frederick the Great becomes ruler of Prussia.

1762—Catherine the Great becomes ruler of Russia.

1775–1783—The American Revolution is fought.

1789—French Revolution begins.

1793–1794—Reign of Terror occurs in France.

1804—Haiti achieves independence from France.

Religion and
Religious Wars

The Trial of Martin Luther

BY LYNNETTE BRENT

K urt walked home along the muddy road. He thought about all the excitement in town. Everyone was talking about what was going to happen to a priest who taught religion at the University of Wittenberg. His name was **Martin Luther**. In 1521 in Kurt's city, Worms, most people were Catholic, just like they were everywhere else in Germany. The Church was having problems with some of its members. Kurt had not really ever thought much about these before now. But now Kurt's head was

---

People and Terms to Know

Martin Luther—(1483–1546) German-born leader of the Protestant Reformation. He wrote books about religion, translated the Bible, formed a system for education, and wrote songs still sung in churches today.

This portrait shows Martin Luther in 1532, when he was nearly 50.

swimming with things he'd just learned. A man was on trial here, in Kurt's town. He was being called a **heretic**.

Kurt turned in at his gate. His thoughts were stopped by his grandchildren's shouts.

"Papa! Tell us what happened today!"

"Yes, Papa. Did you find out more about Martin Luther? Why is he on trial? What did he do?"

His wife, Liese, appeared at the door. "Children, let your grandfather come in and sit down," she scolded. But Kurt could tell that his wife also was eager to hear about the events in town.

"I found out," began Kurt, "that Martin Luther was born not too far from here. His father was a copper miner and very strict. But he gave his son a good education. He even sent Luther to the university to study law."

"But, Papa," interrupted Klaus, "I thought that Luther is a priest!"

"I'm getting to that part. Luther was studying to be a lawyer, as his father wished. Then, one evening, something happened. Luther called it a miracle. While he was walking back to school after

People and Terms to Know

heretic—person accused of heresy, of believing things that go against the teachings of the Catholic Church.

a visit with his family, lightning struck very close to him. Luther was knocked to the ground. At that moment, he called out to Saint Anne and promised to be a monk. Luther kept his promise. His parents were angry with him, but he went to a **monastery** to become a monk."

"So why is he here now at the **Diet of Worms**?"asked Elisabeth. "He must have done something very wrong."

"**Charles V** certainly thinks so. The Emperor called him here. The trouble started in 1510, when Luther first visited Rome. He saw that important people in the Church were not living holy lives. By this time he was a priest and was studying to become a professor of religion here at the University. He was very troubled by the way some of the priests in Rome lived."

"He saw that important people in the Church were not living holy lives."

People and Terms to Know

monastery (MAHN•uh•STEHR•ee)—community or building where monks live.

Diet of Worms—(1521) famous government meeting called by the Holy Roman Emperor Charles V to decide what to do about the problem of Protestantism. It was held in Worms, Germany, where Martin Luther was found guilty of heresy.

Charles V—(1500–1558) king of Spain and emperor of the Holy Roman Empire from 1519 to 1556. His empire included Belgium, the Netherlands, Austria, Spain, and the Spanish lands in the Americas. He belonged to the powerful Hapsburg family.

Kurt continued. "People told me about a letter Luther wrote to the archbishop of Mainz in 1517. The archbishop was selling **indulgences** to raise money for the new cathedral. Luther wrote in his letter that people were getting the wrong impression. They were buying indulgences to 'pay' for their sins and thought this would make sure they went to heaven after they died. Some even thought they did not need to be sorry for their sins and that no sin was too great. Luther said no priest or bishop could guarantee that a person would be saved. Only Christ could do that. And, he said, it was much better for people to do good works than to buy indulgences."

"Ah, yes, that's right," Liese chimed in. "I heard that Luther believes forgiveness comes from being sorry and having faith. They say he doesn't even believe that doing good works will help you get to heaven."

"That's exactly right," continued Kurt. "And what he did about it is what caused all the trouble. In the same year, Luther made a list of all the things that were

---

People and Terms to Know

indulgences—in the Roman Catholic Church, special favors to avoid punishment for sins, both on earth and after death. The Church forbade the sale of indulgences in 1562 at the Council of Trent.

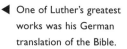
◀ One of Luther's greatest works was his German translation of the Bible.

bothering him about the indulgences and called it the **95 theses**. He nailed this list to the door of Wittenberg Church. That's where many people at the university post notices when they want to discuss ideas."

"Do you know what the theses say?" asked Klaus.

"They are full of new ideas," Kurt responded. "Things like 'the pope cannot remove guilt' and 'indulgences do not bring forgiveness or salvation.' He suggests that the pope and the Church are looking for money rather than people's salvation."

"What did the priests think of Luther's theses?" asked Liese.

People and Terms to Know

95 theses—famous statement of beliefs published by Martin Luther.

"Some holy men support Luther," Kurt replied. "But others, like Johann Eck, oppose him. He and Eck have sent written arguments to each other.

Their supporters have debated each other in public. Our cousin Heinrich, in Leipzig, saw a great debate back in the summer of 1519. He said that Luther argued his beliefs—in public—with Eck. He went further than he had in his 95 theses. He made things worse for himself by saying the pope did not have the last word on matters of religion."

"He is charged with being a nonbeliever, leading others astray, and disobeying the Church's orders."

"What they say about Luther must be true," sighed Liese, "that he just gets into deeper and deeper trouble. What is he charged with?"

"He's on trial here," answered Kurt, "for going against the Church's teachings. The pope **excommunicated** him last January. That's a formal sentence that throws him out of the Church. First they said his teachings broke the law. Now he is charged with being a nonbeliever, leading others astray, and disobeying the Church's orders to take back all that he has said."

People and Terms to Know

excommunicated—formally expelled from membership in the Church.

Kurt noticed that evening was coming on. "It's past time for supper, children. Tomorrow, after I get back from town, I'll fill you in on all the news."

All evening, Kurt was thinking about the next day. He never thought that he'd see anyone question the authority of the Church. Would Luther take back his ideas and admit that he was wrong? Or would he refuse to give in?

The next morning, Kurt hurried down the road to the center of town. He found his neighbor Adolphe already there.

"Were you here early yesterday?" asked Adolphe.

"No, I'm afraid I was working all morning."

"You should have seen it. When Luther came into town, everyone cheered for him. I heard that they cheered him in other towns too. His preaching is supposed to be wonderful. I wonder whether he will take back his teachings when the court asks him to."

Kurt, Adolphe, and many others waited for the news. It came later that day.

Excited bystanders asked each other questions: "What happened in there?" "Is Luther free to go?" "Will he be punished?"

The answer, when it came, raced through the crowd—Luther had refused to take back what he said. In fact, he had very strongly held his ground. He had said, "Unless I am convinced by Scripture and plain reason, I do not accept the authority of the pope and councils, for they have contradicted each other —my conscience is captive to the Word of God. I cannot and I will not recant [take back] anything, for to go against conscience is neither right nor safe. God help me."

_____

"My conscience is captive to the Word of God. I cannot and I will not recant anything."

_____

With that, Luther left. But he wasn't arrested. Instead, Luther was given a letter that allowed him twenty-one days of safe travel home.

Kurt and the others were surprised at what happened next. Charles V issued the Edict of Worms. It called Luther an outlaw and said that anyone who wanted to kill him could do so without being punished for it. However, there were powerful princes in Germany who weren't all in Charles's camp. Kurt didn't know it then, but one, Prince Frederick of Saxony, helped Luther escape and gave him a safe place to stay.

Kurt and his townspeople had witnessed the start of the **Reformation**. What started as a movement to change one church actually caused a brand-new **Protestant** church to be formed. Luther was never put to death. He lived and taught in Wittenberg for most of the rest of his life—preaching, writing, and, with his wife, raising six children.

Other reformers like **John Calvin** and **Ulrich Zwingli** would join the Reformation. They added to and changed some of Luther's goals. But Martin Luther was one of the first who dared to question what many others in Germany and throughout Europe took for granted—the rules made by the Catholic Church.

People and Terms to Know

Reformation—the word means "restructuring or change." In the 1500s, the Protestant Reformation rejected or changed some of the teachings of the Roman Catholic Church. This resulted in the formation of new churches.

Protestant—referring to one of the Christian churches that resulted from the Reformation, such as Lutheran, Baptist, and so on.

John Calvin—(1509–1564) French Protestant founder of Calvinism. He studied religion and law in France and tried to start a government that was based on religious law.

Ulrich Zwingli (ZWIHNG•lee)—(1484–1531) Roman Catholic priest in Switzerland who believed in Martin Luther's ideas. He founded the Reformed Church.

The Table Talk of Martin Luther

The following remarks by Luther were recorded by members of his household:

"In all things, even in the least creatures, and in their parts, God's almighty power and wonderful works clearly shine. For what man, no matter how powerful, wise, and holy, can make out of one fig a fig-tree, or another fig? or, out of one cherry-stone, a cherry, or a cherry-tree? Or what man can know how God creates and preserves all things, and makes them grow?

"The chief cause that I fell out with the pope was this: the pope boasted that he was the head of the church, and condemned all that would not be under his power and authority. . . . With this I could have been content, had he but taught the gospel pure and clear, and not introduced human inventions and lies in its place.

"The pope and his crew can in no way endure the idea of reformation; the mere word creates more alarm at Rome than thunderbolts from heaven or the day of judgment. A cardinal said the other day: 'Let them eat, and drink, and do what they will; but as to reforming us, we think that is a vain idea; we will not endure it.'"

QUESTIONS TO CONSIDER

1. How did Martin Luther's visit to Rome change his thinking?

2. Why did Luther oppose the sale of indulgences?

3. How did Martin Luther share his ideas? What was the result?

4. Why do you think that Charles V handed down such a harsh punishment for Luther?

5. What do you think would have happened to the Reformation if Charles V's sentence had been carried out?

From Soldier to Saint

BY WALTER HAZEN

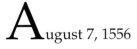ugust 7, 1556

<u>Ignatius Loyola</u>, our founder and superior
general, died one week ago in Rome after a brief
illness. He was 65 years old and had led our organization for over 20 years. Thanks to his dedication
and tireless efforts, the Society of Jesus lives on and
will continue its important work.

As an early member of the Jesuits, I came to know
Ignatius quite well. Let me tell you something
about his life.

People and Terms to Know

Ignatius Loyola—(1491–1556) Spanish-born founder of the Catholic
religious organization known as the Society of Jesus, or Jesuits. The
Jesuits were important in helping the Catholic Church reform itself.

One of the things done by Pope Paul III (upper left) to reform the Roman
Catholic Church was to approve the Jesuit order founded by Ignatius Loyola.

Ignatius was born into an important family. It wasn't anyone's plan for him to lead a religious life. He expected, like other boys of his social class, to become a knight. When he was 16, he became a **page** to the treasurer of the kingdom of **Castile**—a very important person in Spain. Ignatius learned the ways of the court. He became good with a sword. He learned to enjoy gambling and brawling. He also confessed that he liked to flirt with the ladies at court. Soon he became a soldier.

Ignatius's life changed in 1521, when he was 30. In a battle to defend the city of Pamplona against the French, he was badly wounded. A cannonball hit one leg and shattered the other. Because he had fought so bravely, the French did not take him prisoner. Instead, they carried him back to the family castle of Loyola in Spain.

Ignatius's wounds were severe. He would walk with a limp for the rest of his life. While recovering at home, he became bored and asked for something to read. There were only two books available in the castle. One dealt with the life of Christ and the

People and Terms to Know

page—boy who served a knight as part of his own training for knighthood.

Castile—Spanish kingdom that joined with the kingdom of Aragón in 1479 to form a united Spain.

other with the lives of the saints. Ignatius read these two books. They changed his life forever.

Ignatius told me he really preferred to read romance novels. Isn't it strange that the founding of our society came about because there weren't any romance novels in the Loyola castle?

Isn't it strange that the founding of our society came about because there weren't any romance novels in the Loyola castle?

When his leg healed, Ignatius set out on a long journey. The books on Jesus and the saints made him determined to be as much like the saints as he could. He began a long journey to visit Jerusalem, the birthplace of Christ. His first stop along the way was Barcelona. There he planned to take a ship to the **Holy Land**.

Before reaching Barcelona, Ignatius stopped near the town of Manresa. He slept in a cave, intending to stay, he told me, only a few days. But those few days turned into 10 months. During that time, he prayed, **fasted**, and worked at a **hospice**

People and Terms to Know

Holy Land—Palestine, the region where Jesus was born.
fasted—ate little or nothing, often for religious reasons.
hospice—house kept by monks that offered a place of rest for travelers.

in Manresa. He also began to put together the ideas and thoughts that later made up his *Spiritual Exercises*.

Ignatius sailed from Barcelona and reached Jerusalem in 1524. He wanted to preach and help people. He was told, however, that he could not preach because he lacked the proper schooling. In short, he did not know Latin. He would have to learn this language before he would be allowed to serve the Church.

Had it been me, I might have quit. But not Ignatius. He went back to elementary school in Barcelona at the age of 33. He was determined to learn Latin and devote his life to religious work. It didn't seem to bother him that most of his classmates were boys no more than 10 years old. While at school, he supported himself by begging in the streets. He told me that most of his meals consisted of nothing but bread and water.

People and Terms to Know

Spiritual Exercises—famous book of readings, prayers, and meditations written by Ignatius Loyola.

After he decided to dedicate himself to religion, Ignatius Loyola spent seven hours a day in prayer. ▶

Ignatius learned Latin and then moved on to universities in Spain and Paris. His ideas about such things as good works and equal treatment for women attracted followers. They also attracted the attention of the Church. He was warned by Church officials to quit teaching and preaching. When he refused, he was brought before the **Inquisition**. They questioned him and threw him in prison for six weeks. In the end, he was found innocent of all charges.

People and Terms to Know

Inquisition—court established by the Roman Catholic Church to find heretics and get rid of ideas that went against the Church's teachings.

Ignatius told me that prison did not dampen his spirits. Once released, he continued to preach, moving from one city to another. In August 1534, he and six friends, all students of religion at the university, founded our organization. In the beginning, Ignatius called it the Company of Jesus. Each member dedicated his life to God and made three vows, or promises. He promised to lead a life of poverty, to never marry, and to obey God.

He promised to lead a life of poverty, to never marry, and to obey God.

Ignatius summed it up when he said: "We ought always to be ready to believe that what seems to us white is black if the Church so defines it." In other words, strict obedience to the Pope and to the Church was required.

Three years after the founding of the Company of Jesus, Ignatius and his six friends officially became priests. It took some time, but Pope Paul III finally approved of the society in 1540, two years after I joined the order. For the next 15 years, Ignatius led us like an army.

Ignatius Loyola and the organization he founded were unusual. Rather than hide away in some distant monastery and live the life of a lonely monk, Ignatius believed in going out into the world to teach and preach among the people.

Calling ourselves "soldiers of Christ," we set up schools and universities in many places. Our priests went to Africa, India, the Far East, and the newly discovered Americas. It was a time when many were rebelling against the Catholic Church. We helped to keep much of Europe Catholic, and we won back many people who had broken away from the Church earlier. We were successful because we were completely dedicated to our cause. We also were very well educated and trained.

Ignatius Loyola can rest in peace knowing that his Society of Jesus remains strong and dedicated to serving the Church.

QUESTIONS TO CONSIDER

1. What led Loyola to dedicate his life to the service of the Church?

2. Why did Loyola go back to school at the age of 33?

3. What role did the Society of Jesus play in European history?

4. How did the work and activities of the Jesuits differ from those of other religious orders?

The Spiritual Exercises of Ignatius Loyola

Ignatius Loyola's *Spiritual Exercises* are a series of readings, prayers, and meditations that are adapted from the Gospels. Ignatius used *The Spiritual Exercises* to give retreats—times set aside for prayer and meditation. Ignatius felt that his *Spiritual Exercises* would help his followers and others to reach God and to serve Him better.

The Spiritual Exercises are divided into four parts, or weeks. In the first part, a person is to recognize how terrible sin is. In the second part, he or she studies the mission that Jesus carried out while on earth. In the third part, the person thinks about Jesus's death on the cross. In the last part, he or she focuses on Jesus's rising from the dead and return to heaven.

The Society of Jesus still uses *The Spiritual Exercises* today in retreats that its members give for themselves and for others.

Cardinal Richelieu

BY BARBARA LITTMAN

When I first came into the room, I gasped. For a moment, I thought it was **Cardinal Richelieu** back from the dead. But of course it wasn't. The scarlet robe, the matching scarlet hat, the high white collar— they could have fooled anyone, but only for a moment. It was Cardinal Mazarin, whom Cardinal Richelieu chose to follow him. Cardinal Mazarin is here to sign the **Treaty of Westphalia**. Outside, I can

---

People and Terms to Know

Cardinal Richelieu (REESH•uh•LYOO)—(1585–1642) high official in the Catholic Church and chief minister of France under King Louis XIII. He was responsible for policies that eventually broke Hapsburg control of Europe.

Treaty of Westphalia—treaty that ended the Thirty Years' War in 1648. The Hapsburgs and the Holy Roman Empire were on one side, and a number of German princes backed by France, Sweden, and Denmark were on the other. The treaty weakened the Hapsburgs' hold on Europe, and France became the major power in Europe.

Cardinal Richelieu's powerful mind and character appear in this portrait.

hear church bells ringing and people celebrating in the streets.

Today, after thirty years of war, peace has come at last. I had served as Cardinal Richelieu's secretary for more than 10 years when he died. Now, I am Cardinal Mazarin's secretary. It is an honor to be here and see history in the making. How I wish that it could be Cardinal Richelieu sitting at the table. Finally, France is safe. Her borders can no longer be pinched and prodded at every turn by one **Hapsburg** or another. Just as important, inside her borders the king now rules over all. This had been my master's dream.

Many unkind things have been said about my dead master, Cardinal Richelieu. They said he was a liar and a sharp, tricky manager. They said he was cold and without mercy. They said he was an unfeeling charmer who would do anything to reach his goals. Well, there's much people don't know about him. Once you had his trust, he relaxed. In private,

---

People and Terms to Know

Hapsburg—powerful European ruling family. At the height of their power, the Hapsburgs controlled most of Europe, including Germany and Spain and the Spanish colonies in the Americas. Almost all of the Holy Roman Emperors from 1438 on were Hapsburgs.

he never tired of practical jokes. Many times, I felt the playful sting when he took out his pea shooter.

It's true that he would do almost anything to reach his goals. I say, where's the harm? His goals were for the greater good. A strong, unified France was all he ever wanted.

His goals were for the greater good. A strong, unified France was all he ever wanted.

Take his victory at the town of La Rochelle, for example. Now _that_ was certainly a triumph for unity! He broke the power of the **Huguenots** there. I can see him now as clearly as I could that summer in 1627. He ordered the men to dig a ditch, cutting off La Rochelle by land. Then he ordered a **dike** built on the canal that connected the town to the ocean. Completely cut off, La Rochelle could no longer get supplies. By October 1628, when almost three-quarters of its people had starved to death, the town surrendered.

People and Terms to Know

Huguenots (HYOO•guh•nahts)—French Protestant followers of John Calvin. Ever since the Edict of Nantes in 1598, they had had freedom of worship in France and the right to build towns and arm themselves for protection. Richelieu used a Protestant uprising as an excuse to capture their towns and take away their political rights.

dike—low wall built to prevent floods or to dam rivers.

Richelieu had set a powerful example! When royal troops arrived at other Protestant towns, the Huguenots opened the gates. They shouted, "Long live the king and the cardinal!" What surprised other people—but did not surprise me—was that Richelieu continued to give religious freedom to the Protestants. First and foremost, Richelieu wanted loyalty to the Crown.

Now that he had loyalty within France, he knew it was time to turn his attention outside France. War had been going on in the rest of Europe for 10 years. Protestants in Catholic countries wanted to practice their religion without fear. Protestant rulers feared the growing power of the Hapsburgs and the Holy Roman Empire. Catholics were threatened by the increasing number of Protestants. Europe was a boiling pot!

How long would France stay out of it? Not long. Soon after Richelieu's victory at La Rochelle, King **Louis XIII** came to dine. The chef outdid himself that night: roast lamb, baby trout, fresh greens from the garden, and cheese aged to

People and Terms to Know

Louis XIII—(1601–1643) king of France from 1610 to 1643. Basically, Louis let Richelieu, and after him Mazarin, run the country.

perfection. Over dinner, the cardinal presented the king with his views on the state of affairs. I was asked to stay and take notes.

The cardinal argued that France was not safe. The Hapsburgs were pressing in on all sides. One Hapsburg, Philip, ruled Spain to the south. The Netherlands were governed by Philip's aunt. Northern Italy was occupied by Hapsburg Spain. To the east was the Austrian Hapsburg, Ferdinand II, the Holy Roman Emperor. What was to stop Ferdinand II and the king of Spain from uniting to take over France and the Protestant countries in the north? There was nothing, according to Richelieu. Though Catholic, France must join forces with the Protestant countries. It was time to challenge the Hapsburgs.

It was time to challenge the Hapsburgs.

The king and his cardinal began in northern Italy. In 1629, they set out east across the Alps with their troops. Their goal was to reopen the Valtelline Pass. This important pass had been taken by the Spanish in 1620. Quickly, the French troops moved in and took towns in northern Italy, forcing the Spanish out. Many in Europe didn't understand

The Thirty Years' War, 1618–1648

why Richelieu and the king fought against other Catholic rulers. They were outraged and called them traitors.

The king and his cardinal were celebrating. They knew a united, strong France came first. King Louis returned to Paris at once. Cardinal Richelieu took longer, visiting many French towns on his way back. He never missed a chance to make the royal presence felt in all corners of the land.

Soon after, I heard a rumor. This one scared me. Louis XIII was in Lyons and was very ill. People were saying that the king's mother, Marie de Medici, was at his deathbed.

The queen mother was the one who had first brought Cardinal Richelieu to the court. Later, she regretted it. She was a Hapsburg and didn't agree with his policies. I myself never trusted *her*. She was a proud, ill-mannered woman. She spoke in such a high, loud voice, and seemed always to think of herself before others. People who were in Lyons say she tried to scare the king while he was sick. He must stop fighting Catholic rulers, she threatened, or his soul would be lost. If he died, he would spend forever in hell.

Fortunately the king recovered and continued to support Richelieu. When Louis XIII got back to Paris, he went to visit his mother at the Luxembourg Palace. I wasn't there, so I don't know exactly what happened, but this is what I heard.

The king and the queen mother were chatting in one of the drawing rooms. I don't know what they were talking about, but out of the blue, Richelieu appeared. He accused the queen mother of speaking badly of him. She responded by flying into a rage. She screamed at Richelieu. She screamed at the king. She demanded the king choose between her and Richelieu. To ask the king to choose between his own mother and his most trusted advisor: What kind of choice is that?

The king said nothing and went hunting instead. I don't know why, but everyone thought he had chosen his mother. Even Richelieu seemed to think so. But he was wrong. When Marie de Medici heard that her son had chosen Richelieu, she fled the country. She never returned. Richelieu and the king continued to fight the Hapsburgs.

By 1630, the Catholic Hapsburg empire ruled Europe from the Adriatic Sea in the south to the Baltic Sea in the north. France was not the only country afraid of Hapsburg power.

Sweden, to the north, also feared the Hapsburgs. Sweden's ruler, King **Gustavus Adolphus**, was a Protestant. He didn't like the idea of being surrounded by a Catholic empire. Cardinal Richelieu thought Sweden and France should join forces to fight the Hapsburgs. King Gustavus Adolphus wasn't so sure.

Some people called the Swedish king "the Lion of the North," and for good reason. Gustavus Adolphus was strong-willed and had strong

---

People and Terms to Know

Gustavus Adolphus (guh•STAY•vuhs uh•DAHL•fuhs)—(1594–1632) king of Sweden from 1611 to 1632. He defeated the Hapsburgs in three major battles and helped break their hold on Europe.

opinions about everything. Striking a deal with him wasn't easy. Finally he agreed: France would pay Sweden a huge sum each year. Sweden would defend the Baltic Sea.

How could a Catholic country join with a Protestant one to fight the Catholic empire?

Again the Catholic leaders were outraged. How could a Catholic country join with a Protestant one to fight the Catholic empire? Richelieu was surprised when he learned of their reaction. A safe, united France came first. He had always said that. His policy never changed, even if others didn't like it.

As soon as the agreement was signed, King Gustavus Adolphus headed south. Thirty thousand Swedish foot soldiers and six thousand troops on horses were transported across the Baltic Sea. They landed at Stettin and moved inland. To everyone's surprise, Gustavus Adolphus won a major battle at Breitenfeld in Germany. He continued south through Germany, winning more battles along the way. Germany was severely weakened. Hapsburg power was splintered.

Catholic leaders across Europe cursed Cardinal Richelieu. What did he do? Stay up late into the night, with his maps rolled out, planning where to strike next? Yes, I can say he did.

The war lasted another 18 years. Some have said this was the longest, bloodiest war Europe has ever known. Maybe that's so, I don't know. I do know that without Cardinal Richelieu, I would not be standing here behind Cardinal Mazarin. He would not be signing this treaty. The Hapsburg empire would not have been brought down. France would not have new lands and safe borders.

Cardinal Richelieu would have been pleased tonight. He would have been in high spirits. No doubt I would be feeling the sting of his pea shooter. Though much of Europe might find it hard to believe, he liked nothing better than a good practical joke.

QUESTIONS TO CONSIDER

1. What were Cardinal Richelieu's most important goals?
2. What were the reasons the European powers fought the Thirty Years' War?
3. Why was Cardinal Richelieu willing to join with Protestant rulers to fight against Catholic countries, even though Richelieu and his king were Catholic?
4. How did the war make it possible for France to become a leader in Europe?

The Three Musketeers
by Alexandre Dumas (retold by Michael Leitch)

Alexandre Dumas's classic tale of adventure takes place in the France of King Louis XIII and Cardinal Richelieu.

Curse of a Winter Moon
by Mary Casanova

Mary Casanova's historical novel presents a story about village superstition set against the background of the struggle between the Church and the Huguenots in France in the late 1500s.

The Lion of the North:
A Tale of the Times of Gustavus Adolphus
by G. A. Henty

G. A. Henty's historical novel deals with the first part of the Thirty Years' War.

The Glorious Revolution

BY JUDY VOLEM

Nicholas Wood sat on a bench in the shadows of the dark street in Ramsgate, England. It was close to Christmas 1688, but there was no holiday cheer in Nicholas's heart this night. He wasn't sure what he should do next—stay in England or board a ship for the New World. He had to decide by morning.

Nicholas knew that he'd made a big mistake in becoming a clerk for Judge **George Jeffreys**. As badly as he had needed the job, he shouldn't have gotten mixed up in England's religious troubles.

People and Terms to Know

George Jeffreys—(c. 1645–1689) high level minister of law in England. The court sessions held by him after a revolt against James II resulted in so many executions, they were called the "Bloody Assizes."

During the Glorious Revolution of 1688, George Jeffreys, the brutal Lord Chief Justice of England, was caught and beaten by a mob.

The struggle between Catholics and Protestants had been going on for a long time. Ever since King **Henry VIII** left the Catholic Church and set up England as a Protestant country, many people had died in the name of religion. When Henry VIII's daughter **Mary I** became queen, she tried to make England Catholic again. She had so many Protestants killed that she was nicknamed "Bloody Mary."

After Mary came Queen **Elizabeth I**. She was a Protestant. She killed many Catholics trying to return England to the Protestant faith. After her death, the struggles between Catholics and Protestants continued. In the 1640s, England had a bloody civil war. The king was beheaded! England's present king, **James II**, has been working to turn England back into a Catholic nation ever since he came to the throne.

People and Terms to Know

Henry VIII—(1491–1547) king of England from 1509 to 1547. Henry set up the Protestant Church of England.

Mary I—(1516–1558) queen of England from 1553 to 1558. She was the Catholic daughter of Henry VIII and his first wife, Catherine of Aragón, daughter of Ferdinand and Isabella of Spain.

Elizabeth I—(1533–1603) Protestant daughter of Henry VIII. His divorce to marry her mother, Anne Boleyn, began the Protestant Church of England. Elizabeth was queen of England from 1558 to 1603.

James II—(1633–1701) king of England from 1685 to 1688. James's Catholicism and the birth of his Catholic heir caused the Glorious Revolution.

When Nicholas took the job with Judge Jeffreys, the judge was known for his fairness. But shortly afterwards, things changed. King James made the judge Lord Chancellor and gave him great power. The king ordered Jeffreys to frighten, bring to trial, and punish any who disagreed with Catholicism. Jeffreys obeyed, both out of loyalty and out of fear.

The king ordered Jeffreys to frighten, bring to trial, and punish any who disagreed with Catholicism.

A courtroom scene from two years before stood out in Nicholas's mind. The duke of Monmouth's followers were being tried for **treason** after their attempt to over-throw the king. The accused men stood quietly while their wives and children cried, fearing the worst. After all, Monmouth himself had been beheaded, and he was the king's own nephew.

Nicholas remembered the fear he'd felt as he looked at Judge Jeffreys. The judge was dressed in robes that once represented justice. Jeffreys demanded quiet, his eyes red with rage as he looked directly at the accused men. Nicholas

---

People and Terms to Know

treason—high crime against one's country. Spying and other acts of helping enemies are forms of treason.

---

listened and watched with horror as Judge Jeffreys gave his decisions. Hundreds of men were sentenced to hang in those weeks. Eight hundred more were sent into forced labor in the West Indies. There was so much injustice and cruelty, the trials became known as the **Bloody Assizes**.

Nicholas had nightmares for weeks after that. But nothing seemed to bother Judge Jeffreys. He ate and drank heavily and ignored the pleas of the condemned men's families. What had happened to the fair man that Nicholas had known?

Judge Jeffreys was not the only one who had changed. King James also was a different person from when he first came to the throne. His reign had started with great popular support. The people were glad to have a peaceful change from one king to the next after his brother Charles II died suddenly. James promised the nation that he would honor the Protestant Church of England. He called **Parliament** into session, and everyone believed that his rule would follow the laws of the land.

People and Terms to Know

Bloody Assizes (uh•SYZ•uhs)—trials of those involved in the duke of Monmouth's rebellion in 1685. *Assizes* mean "court sessions."

Parliament—in England, the body of government that, with the king or queen, makes up the legislative (lawmaking) branch. It includes the House of Lords and the House of Commons.

But James betrayed the trust of the people. He plotted to bring England under Catholic control, listening to no one but Catholic advisors. Judge Jeffreys went along with all of James's plans to remove Protestants from positions of power and replace them with Catholics, even if it meant killing innocent people.

King James II had only one thought. He would make England Catholic at any cost.

Nicholas remembered with particular horror the trial of Elizabeth Gaunt. She had given shelter and protection to a man accused of plotting to kill the king. The king viewed her act of charity as an act of rebellion. Elizabeth Gaunt was brought before Jeffreys's court. He showed no mercy. Jeffreys ordered her to be burned alive at the stake.

It seemed that King James II had only one thought. He would make England Catholic at any cost. Nothing would stand in his way. Finally, in 1687, he wrote a document that all churchmen had to read and follow. Seven bishops of the Church of England refused to follow his orders, asking the king to take back his letter. He refused. People were horrified when the seven bishops were arrested and led through the streets to the **Tower of London** in chains.

Nicholas had been present at their trial on June 30, 1688. Judge Jeffreys was confident of the king's authority and his own power. But this time the king had gone too far. To Jeffreys' surprise and the relief of the nation, a jury found the bishops innocent. King James's control was crumbling.

Nicholas had joined the people of London as they joyfully celebrated in the streets. Clusters of seven candles burned from house windows in honor of the bishops' victory. James's own troops even joined in celebration. The king had lost the support of the people and his army. He gave up his throne and fled to France.

With King James II gone, Jeffreys had no one to protect him. He knew his enemies would find him. As he was hiding in an inn along the Thames River, an angry mob spotted him and held him. He was taken to the Tower of London, where he was imprisoned for his own safety.

Nicholas looked toward the harbor and sighed. He was too unhappy to stay in England. He boarded a ship to the New World to start a

People and Terms to Know

Tower of London—famous prison in London.

▲
The Glorious Revolution made William and Mary the king and queen of England.

new life. Months later he read about what happened next back home.

The English people had had enough. Seven Protestant leaders wrote to **William of Orange**, asking him to invade England. William agreed and prepared for a battle with James's troops. William landed in western England on November 15, 1688. But no one tried to stop him. Instead, a peaceful, hopeful country, including many of James's own troops, awaited him.

People and Terms to Know

William of Orange—(1650–1702) Protestant ruler in the Netherlands married to Mary, the daughter of England's King James II. Together they were invited by Parliament to become queen and king of England, Scotland, and Ireland. He ruled as William III from 1689 to 1702.

By Christmas of that year, the members of Parliament asked William and his wife, Mary, the Protestant daughter of King James II, to be England's king and queen. They signed the Declaration of Rights that defined their roles and those of Parliament. With the signing of that document, the nation knew that men such as King James II and Judge Jeffreys would no longer have power over the lives of innocent people. In April 1689, Judge George Jeffreys died in the Tower of London.

This change of kings became known as the Glorious Revolution. It was "glorious" because it was completed without a single battle. It marked the end of a terribly violent period in English history and the beginning of a more democratic form of government.

QUESTIONS TO CONSIDER

1. Why do you think that Judge George Jeffreys's behavior changed after his appointment by King James II?

2. Why did the seven bishops refuse to follow the king's orders?

3. What made the Glorious Revolution "glorious"?

4. What does this story show you about how rulers kept power and how they lost it?

The Death of Elizabeth Gaunt

The elderly Elizabeth Gaunt was burned to death for sheltering a rebel against James II. William Penn (1644–1718), who witnessed her death, was the Quaker founder of Pennsylvania.

Mrs. Gaunt was . . . noted for her benevolence which she extended to persons of all professions and persuasions. One of the rebels, knowing her [kindness], had recourse to her in distress and was concealed by her. Hearing of the proclamation which offered [freedom from prosecution for those who gave evidence against others], he betrayed his benefactress and bore evidence against her. He received a pardon as a [reward] for his treachery and she was burnt alive for her charity. One of the witnesses of her death was William Penn, who related that "when she had calmly disposed the straw about her in such a manner as to shorten her sufferings, all the bystanders burst into tears." . . . So died a brave and good woman.

—David Hume, *History of England*

The Enlightenment

Man and Society: Four Views

BY JUDITH LLOYD YERO

Before the 1500s, the Church told Europeans what to believe about the world. During the 1600s and 1700s, people began using their own minds to understand nature and themselves. They moved into a time that many called the Age of **Enlightenment**. This was a time of great advances in science, reason, and human understanding.

People and Terms to Know

Enlightenment—European philosophical movement in the 1700s that emphasized the use of reason to examine accepted ideas. It encouraged many reforms and influenced the American and French Revolutions.

The Ancient of Days, by English artist William Blake (1758–1827), shows a godlike figure, who represents human reason, measuring the universe.

<u>Thomas Hobbes</u>, <u>John Locke</u>, <u>Baron Charles de Montesquieu</u>, and <u>Jean Jacques Rousseau</u> were famous Enlightenment thinkers. They tried to look in a scientific way at why people live together in a society. They also asked questions about the kind of government that people need. They wanted government to be based on sound, natural principles.

These four thinkers couldn't have talked together as they do here because they all weren't alive at the same time. But they would have enjoyed a debate like this one. Based on their writings, we can imagine what they would have said to each other. As you read, decide which of their ideas you agree with. Or perhaps you have a different idea for one or more of them.

People and Terms to Know

Thomas Hobbes—(1588–1679) English philosopher. He argued that people and their government were held together by a social contract. In this contract, people had agreed to give up freedom in order to have protection. He thought a ruler should have absolute power.

John Locke—(1632–1704) English philosopher. He believed that people have a right to end a government that doesn't protect a person's rights to life, liberty, and possessions. Locke's ideas had great influence on America's founding fathers.

Baron Charles de Montesquieu (MAHN•tuh•skyoo)—(1689–1755) French writer who examined different forms of government. He recommended the separation of powers, as well as checks and balances. James Madison argued for using these ideas in the U.S. Constitution.

Jean Jacques Rousseau (roo•SOH)—(1712–1778) French philosopher. He said that people were born equal and argued that society made people unequal. His ideas influenced the leaders of the French Revolution.

HOST: Mr. Hobbes, you argue that people are naturally selfish. Without laws, they will fight to get what they need to be happy and secure. Is this correct?

HOBBES (nodding): People quarrel for three reasons. The first is competition: They invade one another's territory to gain an advantage. The second is distrust: They attack each other out of fear of what the other might do to them. The third is glory: They go to war in order to become famous—to be heroes!

Without laws, they will fight to get what they need to be happy and secure. Is this correct?

Unless people have a strong leader who protects them from each other and from foreigners, they will constantly be at war with one another.

HOST: So you believe that there must be an all-powerful ruler to keep people from fighting? Is that the only reason that they agree to be ruled?

HOBBES: When people are constantly fighting, they have little time for work. They don't explore and don't build. No one has the time to study science, the arts, or literature. Worst of all, they live in constant fear and danger of violent death.

HOST: Mr. Locke, you're shaking your head. What are your thoughts about the basic nature of human beings?

LOCKE: All people should have the right to run their lives as they see fit. Someone else shouldn't tell them what they can and can't do. I disagree with Mr. Hobbes. I believe that people know that it is their duty to love others as they love themselves. If everyone is equal and independent, no one ought to threaten another's life, health, freedom, or possessions.

HOST: So you're saying that I can expect to get what I want from others as long as they can expect the same from me? Why, then, would anyone agree to give up those rights to a ruler?

LOCKE: People join together as a society to help one another protect their lives, liberties, and property. People agree to join in a community for comfortable, safe, and peaceable living and as a greater security against foreigners.

HOST: Baron Montesquieu, do you agree with Mr. Hobbes?

BARON (shaking his head): There's little proof for Mr. Hobbes's claim that people will naturally fight with one another. Mr. Hobbes asks why people go around armed or put locks on their doors if they aren't naturally distrustful. I think it's obvious that this only happens *after* people gather together into a society.

HOST: If you see society as the cause of man's fighting instinct, why do you believe that people form societies?

BARON: At first, people tend to fear strangers. Then they see that the other person is also afraid. In nature, we see animals gathering together in groups. People feel pleasure in the company of others of their own species. Because they can think, people also understand the benefits of living in a community with others.

HOST: Mr. Rousseau, you've been very quiet. Do you believe that people join together into societies because that is their nature? Or do they do it to protect themselves and their property?

ROUSSEAU: Society began with the first man who built a fence around a piece of ground and said, "This is mine." When he found people simple enough to believe him, he opened the door for arguments among them. People would have been spared endless crimes, wars, and murders if only someone had ripped up the fences and said, "Do not listen to this man! Remember that the fruits of the earth are everyone's property and that the land is no one's property!" But by that point things had changed so much that there was no turning back.

"In spite of people's wonderful natures, society has made them dishonest and uncaring."

HOST: You've said that people are, by nature, compassionate and caring. How has society changed that?

ROUSSEAU: In spite of people's wonderful natures, society has made them dishonest and uncaring. There is no wisdom in their decisions. People get pleasure without being truly happy. It goes against the law of nature for the young to rule the old and for fools to rule wise men. It is disgraceful that a privileged few should have so many luxuries while starving people don't have the bare necessities of life.

HOST: Several of you think that governments act in their own interests. They often don't look out for the people's needs. Mr. Locke, what should people do with such a government?

LOCKE: When those in power take away and destroy people's property or make people slaves, those leaders have chosen war. Members of that society no longer have a duty to obey their leaders. People have the right to take back their original liberty. They have the right to set up a new government to give them safety and security. Those are the only reasons that people agree to be governed. And those are the only areas over which people should allow their leaders to have power.

HOST: Baron, you've suggested that one way to avoid this problem is to separate the powers of government. Is that correct?

BARON: You can't have liberty if the same person or group of people has the power both to make the laws and to enforce those laws. People are rightly afraid. Such a ruler or senate can pass harsh laws and then enforce them harshly.

There are worse problems with rulers who have all three powers—to make the laws, to enforce those laws, and to judge those who break those laws. Different branches of the government must hold these powers to prevent abuse.

HOST: Gentlemen, we're running out of time. Does anyone have a final word to those who question your ideas?

LOCKE: I have one observation. New opinions are always questioned. People oppose the ideas only because they are not already common. Society learns and grows only when people consider new ideas fairly and openly.

HOST: Thank you, gentlemen. Your ideas have really made us think.

QUESTIONS TO CONSIDER

1. Who, in your opinion, has the best ideas about why people join in a society and how they should be governed? Why?

2. What evidence can you think of for and against Hobbes's argument that people are by nature selfish and violent?

3. How does separating the powers of government protect the people in a society?

4. When government leaders don't use their power well, what rights do you think people should have?

Gulliver's Travels
by Jonathan Swift (retold by James Dunbar)

Jonathan Swift, like the Enlightenment thinkers, had strong views about the society of his time. He expressed them in Gulliver's Travels. *In this famous story, Swift's hero, Lemuel Gulliver, travels to a series of imaginary places. On these journeys, Gulliver has exciting adventures and learns things about his own society and human nature.*

The Enlightenment
by John M. Dunn

John M. Dunn discusses the origins of the Enlightenment, the important figures of the movement, and their influence.

At the Sign of the Star
by Katherine Sturtevant

Meg Moore is a bright, independent twelve-year-old who lives in London, England, in the 1670s. When her father remarries, she begins a battle of wits with her stepmother. Katherine Sturtevant's historical novel creates a detailed picture of Meg's world.

Voltaire and Frederick the Great

BY MARIANNE McCOMB

The delicious rumor spread from room to room, house to house, and shop to shop. The great **Voltaire** was in prison. Could this be true?

Yes, the rumor *was* true. He was under house arrest at an inn in Frankfurt. The order for his arrest had come from none other than King **Frederick II of Prussia**.

The news came as a great surprise because King Frederick and Voltaire had been friends for many years. In fact, it was Voltaire who first began calling Frederick "Great," and the name

---

People and Terms to Know

Voltaire (vohl•TAIR)—(1694–1778) pen name of François-Marie Arouet, a French writer, historian, and philosopher.

Frederick II of Prussia—(1712–1786) third king of Prussia, who ruled from 1740 to 1786. Frederick the Great, as he was called, made Prussia the strongest military power in Europe during the 1700s.

Voltaire spent much of his life in travel.

had stuck. Frederick, in turn, admired everything about Voltaire and was quick to praise the man for his brilliance.

But still there was no disagreement about the facts: Frederick the Great had arrested Voltaire. Over the next few days, the story slowly came out. Frederick had accused Voltaire of being a thief, and Voltaire had accused Frederick of being a fool. Which of the two men was right? No one could be sure.

* * *

The relationship between Voltaire and Frederick began when Frederick was crown prince, next in line for the throne of Prussia. In 1736, the twenty-four-year-old Frederick sent Voltaire a letter praising his writing. Frederick called Voltaire's works "treasures of the mind" and said that he had been deeply affected by the poet's ideas. Voltaire, who was more than a little bit vain, was flattered by the young prince's praise.

Voltaire's career as a writer had begun shortly after he graduated from the university. His writing style was fresh and witty. He quickly became known for his short, clever sayings. Suddenly, all of Paris wanted to meet him and hear his thoughts.

There was also a serious side to Voltaire. Like many thinkers of the day, Voltaire believed in freedom of thought and religion. He spoke often about his love for freedom and his hatred for those who used power unjustly. He published many of his beliefs in pamphlets that became the talk of Europe.

In one pamphlet, Voltaire said that humans should be guided by reason instead of by religious or moral beliefs. He said that the purpose of life was to achieve happiness by knowing the arts and sciences. He said that the purpose of life was *not* to spend all your time trying to get to heaven.

Voltaire said that humans should be guided by reason instead of by religious or moral beliefs.

In the same pamphlet, Voltaire argued that truly great leaders spend their time building empires rather than tearing down their enemies' empires. Great leaders do not go around seeking wars.

Voltaire's views on the purpose of life and the role of a leader angered many in power. Soon, a warrant was issued for his arrest, and he was imprisoned in the **Bastille** from 1717 to 1718. Later,

People and Terms to Know

Bastille (ba•STEEL)—famous prison in Paris, France.

in 1734 when things became too dangerous for him in Paris, Voltaire fled to the countryside and hid in the home of a friend.

Voltaire continued to be deeply offended by the reaction to his ideas. While in hiding, he felt a loneliness and anger that he had never before experienced. How could people *not* see the value of his ideas?

Voltaire stayed in hiding for more than two years. In the summer of 1736, he received a letter from Crown Prince Frederick of Prussia. Normally Voltaire would have ignored the prince's letter. After all, he had been receiving admiring letters from people for years. But the prince's letter caught Voltaire during a lonely period, so he sat up and took notice.

In his letter, Frederick praised Voltaire over and over again. He ended with a plea for the writer to leave his "ungrateful country and come to a land where you will be adored."

Voltaire read and reread the prince's words. He was thrilled to be so admired. He wrote back and promised to think about this kind invitation to visit.

The prince was overcome with joy when he read Voltaire's letter. In private, the prince confessed that Voltaire was everything he would like to be—cultured, wise, and very popular.

Over the next four years, the two men wrote back and forth regularly. Frederick became Voltaire's most devoted "pupil." For his part, Voltaire continued to enjoy the prince's attentions.

In 1740, Frederick was crowned king of Prussia. He wrote to Voltaire immediately and promised that, as king, he would work for the public good and never forget the lessons that his "teacher" had taught him.

At first, Frederick stayed true to his promises.

At first, Frederick stayed true to his promises. He made laws about religious freedom. He helped the poor. He allowed **freedom of the press**. He ended the use of torture in criminal trials. Voltaire was proud of his "pupil."

During the next ten years, Frederick and Voltaire continued to write. Occasionally Frederick became angry with his role as "pupil" (he was a king now, after all), but he tried not to let his anger show. Sometimes Voltaire also had to hide his feelings about Frederick. It turned out that Frederick was not quite as peace-loving as he first claimed to be. In fact, he waged a bloody eight-year war against Austria

People and Terms to Know

freedom of the press—freedom of writers and newspapers to publish their ideas and views without government control.

and its **allies**. In this war, Frederick and other European powers tried to stop Austria's Maria Theresa, heir of Emperor Charles VI, from taking control of the Hapsburg lands. Voltaire complained to Frederick about his warfare but couldn't quite bring himself to call off their friendship.

In 1750, Voltaire went to the city of Berlin for a long visit. Frederick welcomed him and gave him an elegant set of rooms in the castle. Voltaire enjoyed the luxury of his new life. Dozens of servants fussed over him, and many Prussian princes, princesses, and nobles visited him and hung on his every word. Soon enough Voltaire became the most important person in the Prussian court, aside from King Frederick himself.

Frederick paid Voltaire a large salary for the job of advisor to the king. To earn his salary, Voltaire had to read and comment on Frederick's poetry. As always, Voltaire was brutally honest in his comments. Some of Frederick's poems were worthless, he said, and should be destroyed.

Eventually, Frederick got tired of Voltaire's criticisms. Voltaire sensed that Frederick was

People and Terms to Know

allies—partners, usually by treaty. Allies often join forces to fight a common enemy.

becoming angry, but he ignored it. He was enjoying his life too much to worry how his "pupil" was feeling.

Several years before Voltaire's visit, a man named Maupertuis (moh•pehr•TWEE) was named head of Frederick's Berlin Academy of Sciences. Voltaire became very jealous of Maupertuis and his power. So in 1752 he wrote a short work in which he made fun of Maupertuis and his work.

Frederick was furious. He told Voltaire that any criticism of Maupertuis was a criticism of the king himself. Voltaire refused to apologize. Instead, he secretly sent the work about Maupertuis off to be published in Europe. Soon everyone was laughing at Maupertuis and King Frederick of Prussia.

Finally, Frederick had had enough. He told Voltaire that he must leave Berlin immediately. Voltaire agreed, but only because he had become rather tired of Frederick and his poetry. He quickly packed his bags and headed off—but not before he had grabbed a small booklet of poems that had been written by the king.

When Frederick realized that Voltaire had the poems, he went into a rage. He ordered his guards to arrest Voltaire. His luggage was searched, but the poems were nowhere to be found. Voltaire admitted that he had sent the poems off to Hamburg, Germany.

For more than a month, Voltaire was forced to stay put in Frankfurt, even after the poems were returned. Finally Frederick grew tired of the whole mess and allowed Voltaire to leave.

Voltaire left Frankfurt immediately and promised never to return. When he arrived back in Paris, he told his friends that he would never again speak to the man he had called Frederick the Great.

Eventually, Voltaire and King Frederick calmed down and began writing to each other again. They continued to exchange letters for years to come. But the tone of their letters had changed. Voltaire and Frederick were no longer "teacher" and "pupil." After the incident with the stolen poems, they treated each other as equals: two strong men who knew firsthand the power of the written word.

QUESTIONS TO CONSIDER

1. What kind of man was Voltaire?

2. What was Voltaire's idea about the purpose of life?

3. Why would Voltaire's ideas cause trouble among the people of the 1700s?

4. Why did Frederick the Great admire Voltaire?

5. Would you have wanted to be Voltaire's friend if you were Frederick?

Voltaire's Wit

These examples from Voltaire's writings show why people considered him a great wit:

The secret of being a bore is to tell everything.

Common sense is not so common.

In general, the art of government consists in taking as much money as possible from one class of citizens to give it to the other.

I have never made but one prayer to God, a very short one: "Oh, Lord, make my enemies ridiculous." And God granted it.

Men use thought only to justify their wrongdoings, and speech only to conceal their thoughts.

If God did not exist, it would be necessary to invent him.

He who thinks himself wise, O heavens! is a great fool.

Freedom of thought is the life of the soul.

At the Salon of Madame Geoffrin

BY STEPHEN FEINSTEIN

"**W**hy are you taking me to the house of **Madame Geoffrin**?" I asked my cousin Henri, as our carriage rattled along the cobblestone streets. "I'd much rather walk along the Seine River," I said, "or wander in the palace gardens."

It was a beautiful day in the spring of 1750. The late afternoon sun cast a golden glow on the rooftops of Paris. I had arrived only yesterday, and I was staying at Henri's house. I was eager to see the city's sights.

"Etienne, we can roam around Paris any day," said my cousin Henri. "But today is special. It is

---

People and Terms to Know

Madame Geoffrin (ZHAW•fruhn)—Marie-Thérèse Geoffrin (1699–1777), wealthy French woman who hosted gatherings known as *salons* in Paris. There important philosophers, writers, and artists gathered to share ideas.

This painting of Madame Geoffrin's salon shows her surrounded by philosophers, writers, and artists.

Wednesday. Madame Geoffrin has invited us to her **salon** for dinner—a great honor."

"Well, what is so special about that? Do you mean to tell me she serves food that we cannot find anywhere else?" I asked, impatiently.

"Think of it this way," said Henri. "Madame Geoffrin serves something that is truly unique—food for thought! Every Wednesday, she invites writers and philosophers to her salon for brilliant conversation. She is very interested in the ideas of the day: art, philosophy, literature. You may hear things you have never heard before—things that will challenge your very soul. And by the way, Madame Geoffrin and her guests appreciate witty comments above all else."

> *"Madame Geoffrin serves something that is truly unique—food for thought!"*

"Well, I'm in your hands, Cousin," I said. I began to worry that I might not have anything especially witty or earthshaking to say. Living in the country, as I do, I am not familiar with the latest ideas.

Our carriage stopped in front of a house on the Rue St.-Honoré. "Here we are," said Henri. I adjusted

---

People and Terms to Know

salon—regular gathering of notable people of social or intellectual distinction.

my powdered wig as we got out of the carriage. I wasn't used to wearing a wig, so I carried my three-cornered hat under my arm. Earlier that day, Henri had taken me to one of Paris's 1,200 wig shops. He insisted no gentleman should be seen in public without one. The wig made me look older, and it was too tight and too warm. Also, I didn't much like the fluffy silk shirt with the fancy ruffled sleeves that my cousin insisted that I wear. I might add that I felt naked without my sword. But Henri advised me that it was now the fashion for a gentleman to carry a cane instead of a sword. So straightening my knee-length, scarlet, velvet waistcoat, I followed my cousin into Madame's parlor.

A servant took our hats and canes and led us to the dining room. Loud and lively conversation filled the room. At the head of a very long table sat a woman of about fifty. All of the others seated around her were men. The room grew quiet as we entered. All eyes were upon us. Madame Geoffrin exclaimed, "Henri, my friend, welcome. Who is your dashing companion?" She made me feel comfortable right away.

As soon as I took my first sip of wine, my attention was drawn to the gentleman sitting opposite us. He seemed to be in his late thirties. He spoke with passion about some artist known for his paintings of nudes. He had very strong opinions. "He doesn't know what grace is," he declared. "Delicacy, honesty, innocence, and simplicity have become strangers to him. He has never seen nature for an instant—at least not the nature that interests my soul, yours, that of any wellborn child, that of any woman who has feeling." His voice grew steadily louder, and he grew more excited as he spoke.

What artist could have deserved such an attack from this art critic?

What artist could have deserved such an attack from this art critic? Before I could ask, a white-haired man two seats to my right leaped from his chair and cried, "Who made you the judge of all that is worthwhile in painting, Monsieur **Denis Diderot**? Since you started your *Encyclopedia*, you think you have the last word on every subject under the sun! So now, in

---

People and Terms to Know

Denis Diderot (DEE•duh•ROH)—(1713–1784) French writer and encyclopedist. Diderot's 28-volume *Encyclopedia* (1751–1772) was a famous work of the Enlightenment that helped to shape the reason-based thinking of the time. *Monsieur* is French for "Mister."

addition to literature, politics, economics, religion, and ethics, you are an expert on art. For your information, **<u>François Boucher</u>** is a master in composition, line, and color. He is without question the greatest living painter in France!"

At this, Diderot shouted, "He is without taste!"

"Monsieur," said the white-haired man, "perhaps you would not be so outspoken if Boucher were present this evening."

Before Diderot could say another word, Madame Geoffrin exclaimed, "Ah, there's something good!" Amazingly, this was all it took to quiet the roaring lions.

Henri explained to me that Madame Geoffrin invited Boucher and other artists to her salon on Monday evenings. She felt that it was best not to mix the artists with the writers and philosophers. According to her, only an artist could really understand what another artist expressed in words. "So Monsieur Diderot need not worry that Monsieur Boucher will challenge him to a duel tonight," whispered Henri.

People and Terms to Know

François Boucher (boo•SHAY)—(1703–1770) French painter. His elegant but somewhat artificial work was very popular in his time.

The conversation quieted for a while. The guests politely discussed some books recently published. At the far end of the table, a playwright complimented Henri for his timely guidebook to new theaters of Paris. Now I understood why Henri had been invited. My cousin was a writer!

> "I would sacrifice my life, perhaps, if I could destroy forever the notion of God!"

Dinner came in several courses. First there was an omelette. Then there was some spinach and a small portion of chicken. A good red wine flowed freely. While we ate the chicken, the conversation turned to religion. A philosopher called **Claude-Adrien Helvétius** declared that the Catholic Church had grown too powerful in France. He accused the Church of trying to silence other religions. Being a good Catholic, I was shocked. Helvétius went on to express his hope for a "universal religion," free from rewards and punishments after death.

At this, Diderot cried, "I would sacrifice my life, perhaps, if I could destroy forever the notion of God!" Startled, I dropped my knife on the floor. The critic

---

People and Terms to Know

Claude-Adrien Helvétius (hel•VEE•shuhs)—(1715–1771) French philosopher and conversationalist. He was the wealthy host of a group of Enlightenment thinkers known as *Philosophes*.

spoke against God! At this Madame Geoffrin said, "Gentlemen, that will be quite enough of that! You know I forbid discussions of religion and politics in my salon."

My head was spinning. I didn't know what to think. Did these people like Diderot really mean what they said? After a few more glasses of wine, it didn't seem to matter.

The guests prepared to leave. Madame Geoffrin smiled at me and said, "Well, Etienne, what did you think? You've not said a word all evening."

I had been dreading this moment. I knew I had to come up with a clever comment. Suddenly, an idea popped into my head. "Madame," I said, "I've just had the great pleasure of dining on excellent food for thought!" Everyone in the room nodded in approval—except my cousin Henri. He looked at me with a raised brow, remembering his earlier remark to me.

QUESTIONS TO CONSIDER

1. Why did Etienne begin to worry on the way to Madame Geoffrin's house?

2. What is Diderot's complaint about Boucher's paintings?

3. Why didn't Madame Geoffrin invite artists to her salon the same day she invited writers and philosophers?

4. Why was Etienne shocked by the ideas of Helvétius?

5. If you were one of the guests of Madame Geoffrin, what would you have said?

Catherine the Great

BY CAROLE POPE

Oh, yes, I remember that handwritten note. A messenger delivered it to **Catherine II**, empress of Russia, on July 6th. How I wish I'd been in court that night! Some people said that Catherine had shown no emotion as she read it. Others said she had cried out that her reputation was ruined. The note was from Aleksei, brother of **Grigory Orlov**, one of Catherine's many male friends. Aleksei

---

People and Terms to Know

Catherine II—(1729–1796) German-born princess who became known as Catherine the Great. She was married to Peter III and ruled Russia from June 1762 until her death. After Peter the Great, she is regarded as Russia's greatest ruler.

Grigory Orlov (grih•GOHR•ee uhr•LOF)—(1734–1783) lieutenant in the palace guard who became Catherine the Great's lover, ally, and father of her third child.

Catherine the Great is crowned empress of Russia in 1762.

wrote Catherine that her husband, **Peter III**, had been strangled. "Little Mother, he is no more," the note said. Aleksei pleaded for her forgiveness.

Of course, everyone in court knew that Catherine wanted Peter dead. Why wouldn't she? He was weak and foolish. She had put up with his insults and open hatred for years. Lately, Peter had announced that Catherine was "an idiot" and that he planned to divorce her. He ordered all Russian men to divorce their wives and remarry women he would choose for them. He ordered Catherine to be arrested and thrown into prison.

Peter had finally gone too far. Backed by Grigory Orlov and others, Catherine seized Peter's throne on July 9, 1762, and named herself Russia's sole ruler.

How did Peter react to this news? What would you expect? He panted, sobbed, ran around the palace, fainted, recovered, drank wine, and wrote two orders against her. He made all kinds of bold decisions and then took them back again. Finally, he gave up and **abdicated** the throne. Catherine's followers imprisoned him. Then Peter started sending

---

People and Terms to Know

Peter III—(1728–1762) incompetent, brutal ruler of Russia and husband of Catherine the Great. Peter became Russia's ruler on January 5, 1762, and ruled for about six months until his death.

abdicated—formally gave up power.

Catherine sad notes in French: "I beg Your Majesty . . . to have the kindness to remove the guards from the second room, because the room I am in is so small that I can hardly move in it, and as Your Majesty knows that I always walk back and forth in the room, that will make my legs swell. . . ." The whole court laughed at his notes. He was ridiculous.

Catherine had wanted him dead, to be sure. Did she order his murder?

Catherine had wanted him dead, to be sure. Did she order his murder? Many in court thought that she had. Others said that she hadn't. Many felt that Catherine wouldn't risk being blamed by the Russian people for Peter's death. Anyway, who cared? He was gone.

Catherine had met Peter when she was ten. Young as she was, she thought he was stupid and boring. But her mother, a German princess, wanted Catherine to marry this future ruler of Russia. So Catherine married Peter when she was sixteen and he was seventeen.

The marriage was a disaster. We all could see it. Peter was sickly and childish. He had no interest in ruling Russia. He played with his toy soldiers and

◀ This portrait shows Catherine in Russian costume.

worshiped his mother's enemy, Frederick II of Prussia. Peter did not find Catherine appealing, and she clearly didn't love him. The two were not equals on any level.

Catherine was high-spirited and intelligent. She liked to tell us stories about her childhood. No dolls for her! She liked running and jumping. She even took up bird shooting, a sport that was not for "ladies." She liked to pull up her skirts and walk out into the muddy fields. She was a good shot and let everyone know it.

Though at first Catherine sometimes got down on the floor and played toy soldiers with Peter, she soon gave up on the marriage. Instead, she got to know Russia. She learned the Russian language and studied Russian politics and culture. She was German, but she truly cared about the Russian people. They loved her in return, calling her "Little Mother."

The day she took control of Russia from her husband, Catherine chose not to wear a dress. Instead, she borrowed an officer's uniform, complete with tall black boots and hat. Riding her white horse and leading the soldiers in the procession, she looked glorious. People lined the streets of St. Petersburg that day, joyous with the news. She said of her supporters that day, "The men who surround me are devoid of [lacking in] education, but I am indebted to them for the situation I now hold. They are courageous and honest, and I know they will never betray me."

Now that Catherine's followers had killed Peter, what could Catherine do? Well, she was a practical woman. She put out a statement claiming that he'd died of illness. It turned out that the Russian people didn't care, anyway. They didn't even object when they saw his face in the casket. It had turned black, because he had been strangled.

Now Catherine was free to act to bring peace and good times to Russia. She adored being empress and gave herself completely to the task. First, she set out to improve the country by opening up free trade and building roads. She also cleaned up problems in the government. No one even knew how much money the government had until Catherine found out. Many workers hadn't been paid for months.

Catherine began her rule strongly influenced by the ideas of the Enlightenment thinkers, and she planned great reforms. She took over the Russian Orthodox Church, mostly because she hated its leaders and considered them her enemies. She made the church a part of the government, and the church's property, including its **serfs**, became government property. Then, as head of the state, she freed them, one million serfs in all! Later, however, the French Revolution persuaded Catherine to fear the power of the peasants, and her rule became harsh.

Catherine began her rule strongly influenced by the ideas of the Enlightenment thinkers.

Catherine also followed in the footsteps of **Peter the Great**. She opened up Russia to the outside world, expanding Russia's borders, and welcomed many philosophers and journalists. To prove to leaders of the Enlightenment that Russia was not an ignorant, backward country, she opened schools, a home for orphans, and a public health department.

People and Terms to Know

serfs—workers who could not legally leave the estate of the master they worked for.

Peter the Great—Peter I (1672–1725), ruler of Russia from 1682 to 1725. Peter built St. Petersburg, helped bring crafts and industry to Russia, and opened Russia to influence from Western Europe.

When **smallpox** swept through Russia, Catherine vowed to do something. She brought a doctor from London who was helping to pioneer an **inoculation**. Many people, including myself, were very afraid of this new treatment. To help people overcome their fears, Catherine offered to receive the inoculation first.

Catherine was a fun-loving person who loved the witty atmosphere of court. She awoke each morning, greeted by her many dogs. She drank coffee so strong it would buckle the knees of an ordinary person. To make it, she mixed four cups of water with one pound of coffee! She was bolder than most of us. She tried the potato, which many called the "devil's weed," found it tasty, and encouraged people to grow it.

Catherine the Great was most proud of what she did in the field of law. Over a period of two years, with the help of many people, she rewrote the entire Nakaz, a document that outlined how to revise the legal code.

People and Terms to Know

smallpox—highly contagious, infectious disease caused by the smallpox virus. Smallpox created sores on the skin, shedding of dead skin, and scar formation. Death was often the result.

inoculation—method of introducing a weak, disease-causing virus into the body to protect the body from a more serious case of that or a similar disease.

As time went on, people grumbled about Catherine. Some said she helped the upper class. She sometimes spent money freely. She did not change the condition of Russia's serfs, who remained nearly slaves. She also silenced peasant revolts. But we were proud to be part of her court. She did a great many important things for Russia.

On November 17, 1796, after 34 years as empress, Catherine died. On that day she seemed quite normal and even began to work. But later she was found in bed, barely conscious. She died a short time later. Church bells sadly tolled the news, and all of Russia mourned. We all knew that Russia had lost one of its greatest rulers.

QUESTIONS TO CONSIDER

1. Why was Catherine worried when she received the letter about Peter's death?

2. What is your opinion of Peter III? How would you describe him?

3. What examples of Enlightenment influence on Catherine can you find in this story?

4. In what ways was Catherine great?

Revolution!

Thomas Jefferson

BY LYNNETTE BRENT

I t's New Year's Eve again. When I glance at the calendar, I'm reminded of a special time some years ago. The weather was snowy and cold, and preparations for a wedding were underway. A small group of friends and family were gathering to witness a beautiful moment.

Thomas Jefferson was deeply in love with Martha Skelton. She had become a widow at such a young age. We thought it was wonderful that she had found love again. Their wedding was simple and meaningful. Tom and Martha were a joyful couple.

People and Terms to Know

Thomas Jefferson—(1743–1826) author of the Declaration of Independence and third president of the United States, serving from 1801 to 1809. One of America's greatest thinkers, Jefferson was also a farmer, author, statesman, diplomat, scientist, and architect.

This portrait shows Thomas Jefferson as a young man.

I remember Tom from our school days together. He was not always the great, serious statesman that he has now become. He grew up near the wilderness in Virginia on a plantation called Shadwell that had been started by his father. Tom wasn't exposed to life in the city. However, he was one of the smartest young men I had ever met. His father made sure that his son had a good education. He sent Tom to good schools and hired private tutors. Tom was very well read. When I met him, Tom already had studied Latin with classical scholars.

As brilliant a writer as he later became, he was hardly a speaker.

Tom and I started school at The College of William and Mary in 1760. He was a few years younger than I, starting college at sixteen. His father had died, and Tom decided to enroll in college and live on his own. I remember how young he looked, with carrot-red hair and freckles on his face. He was over six feet tall, but because he bent over, he didn't seem that tall. As brilliant a writer as he later became, he was hardly a speaker. He mumbled, so you had to pay close attention to understand him. Even so, he was very serious about his studies. He quickly learned Greek, French, Italian, and Spanish. He also was a student of philosophy, science, music, and ethics.

Tom's intense studies didn't stop him from having a good time. I remember him saying that he risked being drawn into bad company. Parties, dancing, and horse races always interested him. Fortunately, he learned to steer away from his most troublesome friends and enjoy the company of respectable people.

While at college, Tom gained confidence and developed his speaking skills. He gave up his parties and turned to his studies. Soon he became friends with Dr. William Small, a professor of mathematics and a philosopher. Tom and I went to his lectures on ethics and communication. Dr. Small spent time with Tom nearly every day. Tom grew up under Dr. Small, who introduced him to the ideas of the thinkers of the Enlightenment. Tom began to understand that learning and thinking would open up the whole world to him.

Living in **Williamsburg** also expanded Tom's view of the world. There was a lot going on in Williamsburg. We had a local newspaper, which

People and Terms to Know

Williamsburg—capital of the English colony of Virginia in North America. It was a fine place to learn politics and observe government. Among its grand buildings were the College of William and Mary and the Governor's mansion. Sessions of the colonial legislature met in Williamsburg, as did the General Court.

told us about events all over the colonies. We also were able to go to the theater. The capital of Virginia was located in Williamsburg, too, so Tom and I saw and heard many politicians of the time. We were at the capitol building many times when statesmen debated the rights of the colonies and called for rebellion against British laws.

Dr. Small introduced Tom to the governor of Virginia, **Francis Fauquier**. The governor often hosted gatherings where we would enjoy music and fine food. Dr. Small also introduced him to **George Wythe**, a lawyer who had strong feelings about ethics and patriotism. Eventually, Tom, Dr. Small, George Wythe, and the governor would gather regularly to talk. They would discuss philosophy, the land west of the colonies, and developments in science. Here Tom explored ideas about the rebellion against England that was developing.

People and Terms to Know

Francis Fauquier (FAH•keer)—(c. 1704–1768) English administrator of the colony of Virginia who took an interest in the young Thomas Jefferson.

George Wythe (wihth)—(1726–1806) American lawyer and statesman who was a signer of the Declaration of Independence. He was a mentor to the young Thomas Jefferson.

Dr. Small went to Europe after Tom's first two years at William and Mary, and Tom got a job with George Wythe. Wythe was like a second father to Tom, encouraging him to continue studying languages, history, and literature. Tom's studies would later help him as a lawyer and statesman. Under the direction of Dr. Small, Governor Fauquier, and George Wythe, Tom became a cultured man and a great thinker.

After much study and preparation, Wythe brought Tom into his practice. Tom was a successful attorney, even though he didn't like speaking in front of people. They practiced law together until the Revolutionary War forced the courts to shut down. Tom was elected to represent our county in Virginia and became a representative in the **House of Burgesses**. He was becoming very well known around the colonies.

Then Tom met Martha Skelton. She was the daughter of another well-known lawyer. Tom began courting her in 1771. They would sing together at her family home, The Forest. Tom played violin and Martha played piano. Tom called Martha "Patty" and loved her deeply. He wrote, "In every scheme of happiness she is played in the foreground of the picture, as the principal figure. Take that away, and it is no picture for me."

Tom was deeply involved in the Revolutionary War and the forming of the United States.

They married on New Year's Day of 1772. After the wedding, they took a sleigh ride to the new home Tom was building for her on top of a mountain. The trip covered over 100 miles, and the ground was deep in snow. When they finally arrived, it was the middle of the night. The only room that was complete became their "honeymoon cottage." They lived in that room with all of their furnishings while the rest of the house was being built.

I like to remember that New Year's because it was Tom and Patty's beginning. The years that followed were difficult for them. Tom was deeply involved in the Revolutionary War and the forming of the United States. There also was tragedy at home. Patty's son from her first marriage died. Three months later, she gave birth to their own first daughter. Shortly after that, Patty lost her father.

Tom often was away, so the building of their home went slowly. Patty had six pregnancies while she was married to Tom, but only two of the children lived.

This New Year's Day, Tom is without his Patty. She died in 1782, shortly after giving birth to their sixth child. Still in love with each other, they were reading about the heart and writing poems about their love on her deathbed.

I have called on Tom a few times since Martha died, but his daughter sends me away. Tom is too depressed to see anyone. I only hope that this loss will not break the spirit of the great man that Martha married. Tom has so many talents that this country needs. I can't imagine the United States going on without him.

QUESTIONS TO CONSIDER

1. What did you learn about Thomas Jefferson from reading this story that you did not know before?

2. How did Thomas Jefferson's early years prepare him to become a great leader of the American Revolution?

3. How did Dr. Small influence Thomas Jefferson?

Jefferson and Religious Freedom

When Jefferson was designing his own tomb-stone, he asked that it say: "Here was buried Thomas Jefferson, Author of the Declaration of American Independence, of the Statute of Virginia for Religious Freedom, & Father of the University of Virginia." In the Virginia Statute for Religious Freedom, Jefferson makes a number of points that show the influence of the Enlightenment:

Almighty God created the mind free, and all attempts to influence it create habits of hypocrisy and meanness.

To compel a man to pay money for opinions which he disbelieves is sinful and tyrannical.

Our civil rights have no dependence on our religious opinions any more than on our opinions in physics or geometry.

Finally, truth is great and will prevail if left to herself.

"Let Them Eat Cake"

BY WALTER HAZEN

I shall never forget those six years. In one way, they were wonderful years for France. The **feudal system** ended, and every person became equal under the law. For the first time, we French gained freedom of speech and the press. We also won the right of assembly, which meant we could have meetings without fear of punishment by the government.

But the years between 1789 and 1795 also were terrifying. What violence and bloodshed! The new government beheaded thousands of people at the

---

People and Terms to Know

feudal system—social and economic system in which serfs or peasants worked the land for nobles, who in turn provided armies for the rulers.

Young Queen Marie Antoinette sits in the garden of her palace.

guillotine. Two of them were the king and queen. Their deaths ended the **monarchy** in France.

Let me introduce myself. My name is Armand. During those awful years of unrest, I was a minor official at the court of **Louis XVI**. While at court, I had seen and heard things that troubled me. I sensed that sooner or later something terrible was going to happen.

I will begin my story by telling you something about my king. Frankly, Louis did not look or act like a king. He was clumsy and he paid little attention to his appearance. He cared more for hunting than ruling. As a youth, he had liked to talk to and work with the various skilled workers at court.

Frankly, Louis did not look or act like a king.

He was surprisingly strong, too. I once saw him lift a young man with one arm.

Louis XVI was a nice man, and he had a good heart. But he was a weak ruler at a time when a strong leader was needed. France was going

---

People and Terms to Know

guillotine (GEE•uh•teen)—machine that uses a heavy falling blade to execute people by chopping off their heads.

monarchy—form of government headed by a king, queen, emperor, or similar ruler.

Louis XVI—(1754–1793) king of France from 1774 to 1792. Louis was king when the French Revolution began in 1789.

through a troublesome period. Because of wasteful spending—partly by Louis's queen, **Marie Antoinette**—the government was in debt. France's social classes were divided, too. The nobles and the church officials had all the power and enjoyed special rights. They paid no taxes and held all the important positions in the government. The peasants, or poor farmers, had little. At times they starved. The government could make them work without pay on roads, bridges, and other projects. Through the years, I had watched these people become increasingly restless and angry.

Another problem facing the king was a growing **middle class**. It had become quite large because of an increase in trade and business. Its members believed that the nobles and the clergy should give up their special privileges. From this class came the leaders of the **French Revolution**.

People and Terms to Know

Marie Antoinette—(1755–1793) Austrian princess who married France's King Louis XVI in 1770. She was the daughter of the Hapsburg ruler Maria Theresa, the empress of Austria and queen of Hungary.

middle class—class between the very wealthy and workers without special skills. Merchants and businessmen are part of the middle class.

French Revolution—political upheaval that began in France in 1789. This revolution overthrew the monarchy and brought democratic changes to France.

Marie Antoinette definitely made things worse for Louis. Few people liked her. As queen, she was empty-headed and, as I said earlier, she was very wasteful when it came to spending.

How wasteful was she? Well, here's an example. One time, she had the king build a little village of farmers' cottages on the grounds of the royal palace at **Versailles**. Why this make-believe village? So she and her favorites at court could dress up like peasants and play at being milkmaids and shepherds! Marie Antoinette also gambled at the horse races and threw fancy parties. I heard that she had been spoiled as a child in Austria. She always got what she wanted by throwing a fit. We at court guessed she used the same method to get what she wanted from the king.

The queen also meddled in the business of government. She talked Louis into giving jobs to her favorites. Neither she nor Louis understood what was happening in their country. That was obvious. The whole court heard about a conversation she had with a court official one day. "Why are the people of Paris so angry?" the queen asked.

"Because they have no bread," came the reply.

People and Terms to Know

Versailles (vuhr•SY)—very grand royal palace just southwest of Paris.

"Then let them eat cake!" the queen was supposed to have said.

Whether the queen actually made that statement is not important. What is important is that people throughout France believed she was capable of anything. They even believed she was a spy for Austria, our old enemy. People loved the king, in spite of his weaknesses. But they didn't love her.

> *People loved the king, in spite of his weaknesses. But they didn't love her.*

Matters in our country came to a head in 1789. In that year, with the government badly in debt, King Louis XVI decided to call a meeting of the **Estates-General**, our national legislature. This body had not met since 1614. But Louis was desperate. He needed money, and the courts had refused to sign his orders to increase taxes. For that reason, he called the representatives of the Estates-General to Paris.

Louis was not prepared for what happened. Representatives of three estates or classes—the clergy, the nobles, and the common people—came

---

People and Terms to Know

Estates-General—French national assembly from 1302 to 1789. It was made up of representatives from the three estates, or classes: the clergy (church officials), the nobility, and the common people. It approved laws the king made, but did not make laws itself.

to the meeting. Louis thought that they would vote as they always had. Each estate as a group usually had one vote. The clergy and nobles, who made up the first two estates, usually outvoted the third estate, the common people, two to one. So the common people never got control.

But this time, the third estate, representing the common people, had other ideas. They demanded that each representative have one vote. Since they were the largest group, they would be in the majority. They could outvote the clergy and nobles and bring about much-needed changes.

Faced with this problem, Louis had the representatives of the third estate locked out of their meeting place. But they were not discouraged. They met on a tennis court and invited the nobles and clergy to join them. Then, on June 20, 1789, they took a famous oath, called the Tennis Court Oath. They promised not to leave until they had given France a written constitution. With this, the king gave in and ordered the three estates to sit together and vote as individuals. This was a historic change.

Everything was fine for several weeks. The Estates-General grew into the National Assembly and set to work to bring about needed changes.

▲
Louis XVI gives orders to the leader of a group of French explorers.

Then Louis XVI did a foolish thing. He gathered some troops around him at his palace at Versailles. The people of Paris thought he planned to stop the work of the National Assembly. On July 14, a mob, looking for weapons, stormed the Bastille, a prison where people who had spoken out against the king were held. They killed the guards and freed the prisoners.

The taking of the Bastille was the first act of violence of the French Revolution. Others soon followed. Peasants in the countryside burned the homes of nobles. They destroyed property and records. Many nobles, fearing for their lives, fled to other countries. I was as terrified as anyone else. I was only a minor official, and I hoped that I wasn't in danger. But I took no chances. I sent my wife and child to live with relatives in the south.

The violence that began at the Bastille caused Louis XVI to accept the National Assembly as the new government. Oh, if only the revolution had ended there! The National Assembly passed laws that brought democracy to our country. Some laws ended the special privileges of the upper classes. Other laws provided for individual freedoms and liberties. Most important, a constitution was written and approved. It allowed Louis XVI to keep his throne, but it took away many of his powers. He became a **limited monarch**, much like the rulers of England.

But, no, the revolution continued. One reason was that the king made another mistake. In June 1791, he and his family tried to leave France. Caught at the border, they were brought back to

---

People and Terms to Know

limited monarch—ruler whose powers are restricted by law.

Paris. As time went on, the revolution began to take a nasty turn. The National Assembly was replaced by a new group of representatives and was called the Legislative Assembly. This group was replaced by a more extreme group called the National Convention.

During 1793 and 1794, France suffered through the Reign of Terror. Everyone in the upper classes feared for their lives. The men who controlled the National Convention began to kill everyone they thought opposed the revolution. The guillotine never stopped. Crowds gathered to watch the almost daily beheadings. Some thought of it as entertainment. On January 21, 1793, the king himself was beheaded. Marie Antoinette died the same way. She was led to the guillotine on October 16 of that year.

The guillotine never stopped. Crowds gathered to watch the almost daily beheadings.

No one knows for certain how many people died at the guillotine. During one period of 47 days, nearly 1,400 people were beheaded. I also have heard that the total number beheaded may have been as high as 20,000. I can't believe that I survived.

By 1795, the French people had had enough bloodshed. The National Convention was replaced, and the executions ended. In spite of the terror, France had seen tremendous changes in a short time. One of the last of the **absolute monarchies** in Europe was overthrown and the feudal system was brought to an end.

QUESTIONS TO CONSIDER

1. What conditions in France led to revolution in 1789?

2. What was the Tennis Court Oath?

3. What event caused the revolution to take a more violent turn?

4. Based on what happened in the French Revolution, what advice would you have given Louis XVI and Marie Antoinette?

People and Terms to Know

absolute monarchies—governments by kings or similar rulers who have unlimited power.

Life During the French Revolution
by Gail B. Stewart

Gail B. Stewart covers both the political events and the social history of the period of the French Revolution.

Helen Williams and the French Revolution
by Helen Maria Williams (edited by Jane Shuter)

Helen Maria Williams was an Englishwoman who lived in Paris during the Reign of Terror. Her letters provide an account of this violent period of the French Revolution.

A Tale of Two Cities
by Charles Dickens

Charles Dickens's classic novel begins in the years leading up to the French Revolution and reaches its climax in the Reign of Terror.

Toussaint L'Ouverture

BY BARBARA LITTMAN

<u>T</u>oussaint L'Ouverture lay on the narrow bed in a mountain fortress high in the French Alps. He was feverish. Every bone in his body ached, and he was racked with fits of uncontrollable coughing. Even with the small fire he had started, the room was bone-chillingly cold. The four-foot-thick stone walls sucked up the heat and were still clammy. Little light made its way into the damp and chilly room—really a prison cell. The windows had been almost completely bricked up.

Memories drifted in and out of his foggy brain. He recalled a library, a kindly priest reading him a

---

People and Terms to Know

Toussaint L'Ouverture (too•SAN loo•vehr•TYOOR)—(1743–1803) Haitian slave who became the leader of Haiti's successful attempt to gain independence from colonial rule.

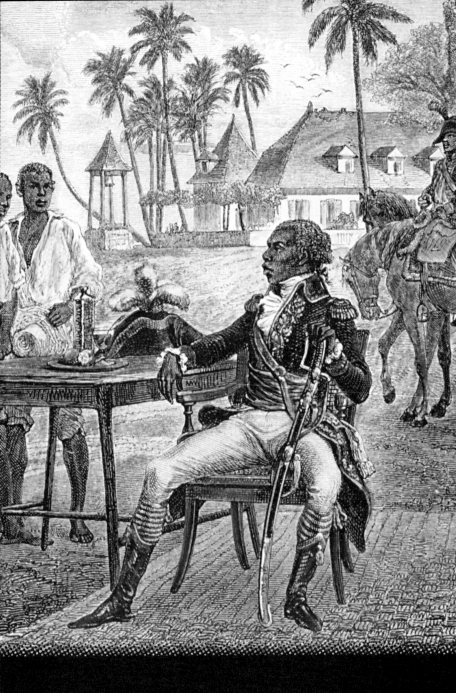

Toussaint L'Ouverture is shown wearing his military uniform.

story. Were these the deathbed visions of a sick, weary man? Toussaint remembered a strong, white hand reaching toward book-heavy shelves. That was the hand of Bayon de Libertad, his master. Libertad had treated his slaves well and had taken a special liking to Toussaint. He had encouraged Toussaint to read and think for himself. By the time Toussaint was in his twenties, Libertad liked nothing better than to have lively discussions with this intelligent, educated slave.

Still in a feverish fog, Toussaint could hear the voice of Father Baptiste. It sounded just as it had over 50 years ago, when was a young boy. One more time, Father Baptiste was telling him the story he loved more than any other—the story of Spartacus. Spartacus had been a slave also, just like Toussaint. Yes, Spartacus had been white. Yes, he had lived in Rome almost 2,000 years ago. But to Toussaint, he was like a brother.

Spartacus had led a successful slave rebellion against his Roman masters. Toussaint had done the same against the white slave masters of **Haiti**. Now

---

People and Terms to Know

Haiti—today, a republic in the West Indies on the island of Hispaniola. (The Dominican Republic is also on this island. The West Indies is a long chain of islands between Florida and South America.) Haiti was controlled by the Spanish from the 1500s until 1697. Then it was controlled by the French. Toussaint L'Ouverture led a slave revolt that eventually gained Haiti its independence in 1804.

he was lying in this foul-smelling, cold, damp cell more than 3,000 miles from home because that French devil, General **Charles Leclerc**, had tricked him.

Time and time again Toussaint and his slave rebels had outsmarted Spain, England, and France—three of the most powerful countries in the world. England would have liked to own part of the island Toussaint called home. France and Spain already each owned part of the island but would have liked to own more. Haiti was the wealthiest European colony in the Americas. It provided almost half of Europe's coffee, sugar, and cotton.

Time and time again Toussaint and his slave rebels had outsmarted Spain, England, and France.

Its wealth came at a price, and enslaved Africans paid the price. After an ocean voyage packed into the overcrowded, filthy hold of a cargo ship, the slaves arrived sick, hungry, and scared. Once they were sold at auction, field slaves worked in the plantation fields from sunrise to sundown. Those who disobeyed or stopped working were whipped

---

People and Terms to Know

Charles Leclerc (luh•KLER)—(1772–1802) French general and brother-in-law of Napoleon, whom Napoleon appointed to lead the French invasion of Haiti after Toussaint and his followers beat the English and Spanish.

until the skin on their backs bled. Many slaves were so hungry, they often sneaked out at night to raid gardens and other plantations.

It's true that there were laws that were supposed to protect the slaves. But white slave owners ignored them, and nobody tried to enforce them. The slaves were at their masters' mercy. Many slaves were so unhappy that they killed themselves.

Slaves were not the only group on Haiti that was unhappy. The white plantation owners didn't like French rule. They were allowed to sell their goods only to France. France turned around and sold the same goods at a high profit to the rest of Europe. The white city dwellers were envious of the plantation owners' wealth. And most whites envied the mulattos—the children of one white parent and one black parent. In Haiti, mulattos were free men and often very wealthy. They were some of the wealthiest plantation owners on the island. Yet their wealth did not make up for their lack of rights. They wanted full citizenship. All this discontent was heightened by news of events in France.

Toussaint twisted and turned in his sickbed, trying to get comfortable. Three words were going through his head over and over again: *liberty, equality, and fraternity.* This had been the battle cry of the French Revolution. It was the summer of 1789. All around him, there was talk of the revolution in France. France's last king, Louis XVI, had been overthrown. Toussaint and the other slaves heard their white masters talk heatedly about the "**Declaration of the Rights of Man**."

Revolution was like a wave. First came the United States of America, whose revolution against colonial rule began in 1776. Around the world,

Revolution was like a wave.

people watched as American revolutionaries freed themselves from English rule. Then, little more than 10 years later, the world watched as **Maximilien Robespierre** and others overthrew the French king. Could Haiti be next? There was certainly enough discontent. The whites wanted freedom from French taxes and trade rules. Mulattos and free blacks wanted the rights of full citizenship. Black slaves wanted their freedom.

People and Terms to Know

"Declaration of the Rights of Man"—charter of rights and liberties adopted by the French National Assembly in 1789.

Maximilien Robespierre (MAK•suh•MIHL•yuhn ROHBZ•peer)— (1758–1794) extremist leader of the French Revolution who eventually was executed.

In his feverish mind's eye, Toussaint could see the flames that began their revolution on August 12, 1791. For days before, slaves had gathered deep in the Alligator Wood, chanting, dancing, and planning their revenge. The mysterious **Boukman** was the leader. This huge, powerful slave had the important posts of coachman and field commander at his plantation. This helped him to organize a revolt. His plan: at the same time, all across the island, in the dark of night, thousands of slaves would set fire to plantations and cities.

Within days, 2,000 whites were dead. Hundreds of sugar and coffee plantations were destroyed. For days afterward, slaves continued their revolt, murdering and torturing whites as they themselves had been tortured for so many years.

Toussaint hadn't helped plan the revolt. In fact, all he could see now through the imagined smoke were the frightened faces of his kind master and mistress. Toussaint believed they should not suffer the fate of cruel slave masters. To save their lives, he had whisked them into a wagon and driven as fast as he could to the coast. From there, they escaped to America.

People and Terms to Know

Boukman—(died 1791) Jamaican-born slave and priest of an African religion who was an important leader of the Haitian slave revolt. Self-educated, Boukman always carried a book, and got the nickname "Bookman."

When Toussaint returned to his plantation, it was a smoking ruin. Even though his master had been kind, Toussaint knew he was the exception. Remembering his favorite tale about the Roman slave Spartacus, Toussaint joined the revolt.

As cold and tired as he was now, Toussaint couldn't help but smile. His army of rebels had been a ragtag group. Often dressed in rags, they outfoxed the white plantation owners and highly trained French troops. The rebels always avoided a head-on battle with their enemy. Usually, they would try to lure the enemy onto high ground where the whites weren't used to fighting. Then, Toussaint's rebels broke into small groups on horseback and zigzagged through the trees and bushes. Their opponents thought there were more of them than there were. Sometimes women and children would weave in and out of the bushes, singing and dancing. Then all of a sudden, they would stop. Small bands of about 10 men would be right behind them, creeping flat along the ground. The eerie singing and dancing scared and confused the white islanders and French soldiers. Just when they were most confused and scared, the small bands would attack.

The eerie singing and dancing scared and confused the white islanders and French soldiers.

Toussaint quickly earned a reputation as a great general. He earned his last name, L'Ouverture, from his military skill. Toussaint became so good at breaking open the lines of French troops, people started to call him "the opener," or in French, "L'Ouverture."

For more than a year, battles raged, mixed with efforts on both sides to strike a deal for peace. Little progress was made, though. The plantation owners wanted the slaves to return to work. They promised to treat the slaves well, but Toussaint and the other generals knew better.

At the time that Toussaint was waging his slave rebellion, tension between the mulattos and whites was growing. The French National Assembly had recently voted to give citizenship to all property-owning, free men of color. A civil war broke out in the southern part of the French colony. Now the National Assembly had to act to do something to turn things around.

His thoughts turned to Sonthonax. Toussaint would never forget that name. What a strange turn of events had eventually given the slaves their freedom.

Three new commissioners were sent to the colony. It was their job to straighten things out and enforce the new law. Of the three, Sonthonax proved to be the most important.

During his first year in Haiti, Sonthonax began to get the slave rebellion and civil war under control. It looked like Haiti would remain a loyal French colony. Then disaster struck. France declared war on Britain, and the French revolutionary government beheaded King Louis XVI. The white colonists heard that their king had been murdered. Many wanted independence from the new revolutionary government in France. They turned to England for

▲
Workers press sugar cane in a mill.

help. For control of such a rich island, England was only too glad to supply troops.

Many slaves also lost hope of freedom under the revolutionary government of France. It had killed the king who had given citizenship to free men of color. Large numbers of slaves fled to the Spanish part of the island.

Toussaint thought about the 6,000 troops the French commissioners had brought with them. Six thousand troops was laughable. It was too small a number to go up against the British and to fight off the Spanish, whose numbers were now swelled with the newly arrived slaves. He laughed, then wished he hadn't. The laughter brought on a fit of coughing. . .

Sonthonax did the only thing he could. He freed all the slaves of Haiti. It was a gamble he had to take. He hoped that the slaves—500,000 of them—would want to become free French citizens. If they did, then he would have the troops he needed to fight off the English invasion.

Little by little, slaves trickled over to the French side. Then, on January 24, 1794, Toussaint also joined the French. With him came his men and the methods they had once used so successfully against the French. The tide was turned. They lured the British to high ground. They scared and tricked them into believing there were more of them than there were. Soon the Spanish signed over their part of the island to the French. Then Britain withdrew. Their troops were discouraged, and a serious rebellion was brewing in Jamaica. It needed their attention.

Toussaint's chest ached from all the coughing. Even though he could tell his fever was higher, he was racked with chills. For all he had done for Haiti, was this the fate he deserved? Too weak and tired to feel real anger, he cursed Leclerc.

For all he had done for Haiti, was this the fate he deserved?

Napoleon was worse. He had praised Toussaint for all he had done to save Haiti from the British and Spanish. Yet, at the same time, he had given Leclerc secret orders. He was to capture Toussaint L'Ouverture, make him a slave again, and cancel Haiti's new constitutional government. From a spy, Toussaint had learned that Napoleon was sending troops

---

People and Terms to Know

Napoleon—(1769–1821) famous French general and conqueror who was emperor of France from 1799 until 1814, when he was exiled. He regained power for a short time during 1815, and then was exiled again.

---

and planned to invade. When Leclerc landed in January 1802, Toussaint was prepared. For months, Toussaint and his rebels fought Leclerc. Both had heavy losses. Finally, the two leaders agreed to meet to discuss a settlement. Leclerc guaranteed Toussaint's freedom. But he lied. The French leader lied, and that is why Toussaint lay dying in this cold fortress in the mountains.

*　　*　　*

Toussaint L'Ouverture died in April 1803, but his cause did not die with him. His men continued to fight. In November of 1803, they captured the last city occupied by the French. Like its neighbor to the north, the United States, Haiti won independence from its colonial ruler and became the first independent black republic in the world.

The Haitian revolt changed the course of history in many ways. Because of it, Napoleon gave up on establishing an empire in the Western Hemisphere and sold the vast French colony of Louisiana to the United States. During the revolt, many Haitian refugees fled to the United States, greatly influencing the culture of the southern

United States. The revolt also helped move the United States toward the Civil War. Inspired by the Haitians' success, American slaves tried unsuccessful revolts of their own in South Carolina and Virginia. This terrified American Southerners, who began to fear that ending slavery meant a race war. But antislavery groups in the North became even more sympathetic with the downtrodden slaves in their own nation.

QUESTIONS TO CONSIDER

1. What were the reasons that each of the three groups in Haiti—black slaves, whites, and mulattos—were unhappy?

2. How did the French and American revolutions influence events in Haiti in the 1790s?

3. How did Toussaint and his rebels beat their enemies?

4. Why did Sonthonax free the Haitian slaves?

5. Why do you think Toussaint L'Overture is important in world history?

Toussaint L'Ouverture:
The Fight for Haiti's Freedom
by Walter Dean Myers

In the 1940s, the African-American artist Jacob Lawrence did a series of 41 paintings that retold the story of Toussaint L'Ouverture. In this book, Lawrence's paintings have been joined with a text by the African-American writer Walter Dean Myers.

Black Patriot and Martyr: Toussaint of Haiti
by Ann Griffiths

Ann Griffiths' biography gives a complete account of the life and achievements of Toussaint L'Ouverture.

Rebels Against Slavery:
American Slave Revolts
by Patricia C. McKissack and Frederick L. McKissack

The McKissacks describe the slave revolts in the United States that were inspired by the example of Toussaint L'Ouverture.

Invention and Discovery

Tomatoes Are Poison and Potatoes Cause Leprosy

BY DEE MASTERS

Fresh from victories in what is now Cuba, in February 1519, the Spanish soldier-adventurer **Hernán Cortés** sailed to Mexico with an army of 600 men.

Cortés and his men marched toward **Tenochtitlán**, the wealthy capital city of the ruling Aztec Indians. Thousands of Indians who hated the Aztec rule joined Cortés. They were in awe of the Spaniards' horses and metal weapons. Many

---

People and Terms to Know

Hernán Cortés (ER•nahn kahr•TEHZ)—(1485–1547) Spanish conqueror of Mexico. When Cortés arrived in Mexico, he established a city called Vera Cruz and burned his ships to prevent his soldiers from trying to go home.

Tenochtitlán (tay•NOCH•teet•LAHN)—Aztec capital under Montezuma, center of an advanced civilization. It covered more than five square miles with 140,000 people, an elaborate guild system, and a thriving economy.

Millions of American Indians died of smallpox, which reached the Americas with the European explorers.

believed Cortés to be Quetzalcoatl, an Aztec god. When the Spaniards arrived in the capital, **Montezuma**, the Aztec emperor, sent messengers to welcome them. But Cortés suspected a trap and imprisoned the emperor as a hostage. Later, the Aztec people started to believe that Montezuma was working with the conquerors. They rebelled, killing him and driving Cortés and his men from the city. In May 1521, Cortés returned with several thousand Indians and about 1,000 Spaniards and by August took the city. Within a few months, Cortés also controlled central Mexico. Cortés was the conqueror of the Aztecs!

Smallpox had conquered the Aztecs.

Only, he wasn't their conqueror. In fact, smallpox had conquered the Aztecs. When the Spanish army first arrived, a black soldier was suffering from smallpox. As Bernal Díaz del Castillo, a soldier with Cortés, tells the story, this black man "infected the household where he was quartered; and it spread from one Indian to another, and they being so

---

People and Terms to Know

Montezuma (mahn•tih•ZOO•muh)—Montezuma II (1456–1520), Aztec emperor of Mexico. Montezuma controlled a vast and wealthy empire that included today's Honduras and Nicaragua. His palace covered 10 acres and had 300 rooms.

numerous and eating and sleeping together, quickly infected the whole country . . . it was because of him that the whole country was stricken with a great many deaths."

In the 60 days after Cortés was driven from the city, the **epidemic** spread. When the Spaniards returned and attacked, the Aztecs put up a strong defense, considering they were dying of smallpox and pneumonia. After nearly three months, the Aztecs surrendered. Official letters from Cortés's forces say that when the city fell, "the streets, squares, houses, and courts were filled with bodies, so that it was impossible to pass. Even Cortés was sick from the stench in his nostrils."

An Indian account of what happened inside the city gives a clearer picture:

"It was the month of Tepeilhuitl when it began, and it spread over the people as great destruction. Some it quite covered with sores on all parts—their faces, their heads, their breasts, all over. There was a great havoc. Very many died of it. They could not walk; they only lay in their resting places and beds.

People and Terms to Know

epidemic—rapid spread of an illness, usually affecting many people.

They could not move; they could not stir; they could not change position, nor lie on one side; nor face down, nor on their backs. And if they stirred, much did they cry out. Great was its destruction. Covered, mantled with sores, very many people died of them." Those who survived were permanently scarred. Some went blind.

Why did so many more Indians than Spaniards die of smallpox? Many of the Spaniards had already had the disease when they were children and could not get it again. Generations of their ancestors had had smallpox and had passed down a tolerance for it. Smallpox was an Old World disease. The Indians didn't have a built-in protection to it. For them, smallpox, measles, and many other common European diseases did not exist until 1492. In *The Book of Chilam Balam*, a conquered Yucatan Indian wrote, "There was then no sickness; they had no aching bones; they had then no high fever; they had then no smallpox; they had then no burning chest; . . . they had then no headache. At that time the course of humanity was orderly. The foreigners made it otherwise when they arrived."

Smallpox was just one item in the trade between the New World and the Old we call the **Columbian Exchange**, and it is still going on.

Columbus did not discover the Americas. He wasn't even the first European to reach the New World. What makes 1492 so important is that, after that date, the continents were in continual contact and trade. People who crossed the oceans brought with them vegetables, fruit, animals, seeds, and diseases.

What makes 1492 so important is that, after that date, the continents were in continual contact and trade.

The Europeans brought horses, cattle, pigs, oxen, and rats. Some of these escaped and became more plentiful than native animals. In fact, sometimes they caused the native animals to die out.

The Europeans brought rice, wheat, grapes, cauliflower, cabbage, radishes, lettuce, oranges, lemons, bananas, and sugar cane. By 1610, Brazil alone was producing 57,000 tons of sugar. The sugar cane plantations set the model for other large

People and Terms to Know

Columbian Exchange—transfer of plants, animals, and diseases between the Western Hemisphere and the Eastern Hemisphere that began with Columbus's first voyage.

plantations. Eventually, there were tobacco (another New World plant) plantations in Virginia. Europeans didn't like working these large plantations in tropical areas. So they brought millions of black African slaves to the New World to work on the plantations for them. Soon the black slaves outnumbered the European settlers.

The Columbian Exchange went both ways. European diseases swept through the American Indian population. But a tiny organism, *Treponema pallidum*, or syphilis, seems to have come from the Americas and spread through Europe. Before Columbus died, European sailors carried the disease to every continent except Antarctica and Australia. Unlike smallpox, syphilis sores were large, so it was called the Great Pox. The disease was so awful that its name became a curse: "A pox on you!"

Syphilis was a terrible curse. Small, open sores gave way to a general rash. As the disease spread, parts of the body often would rot away. Large tumors appeared, and the victims suffered horrible pains in muscles and nerves. Bones would be eaten away. Hair and teeth would drop out. Often the sick person would lose his or her eyesight and might eventually go crazy from nerve damage. When syphilis first arrived in the Old World, most of its victims died.

As the Columbian Exchange brought death, it also brought life. Old World rice and wheat became basic foods for the New World's growing population. But the largest growth in population came because the Old World received New World vegetables: corn, potatoes, sweet potatoes, **manioc**, and American beans.

As the Columbian Exchange brought death, it also brought life.

The new plants were not always quickly accepted. At first, some Europeans believed that tomatoes were poisonous and potatoes caused **leprosy**.

But the potato quickly became the main food of the European poor. The Irish poor were the first to make it the main part of their diet. Many poor Irish ate ten pounds of potatoes a day and almost nothing else. With the potato as a food source, the population of Ireland grew from 3.2

People and Terms to Know

manioc (MAN•ee•ahk)—root crop that came from South America. It grows well in damp, hot areas.

leprosy—disease of the skin, flesh, and nerves which results in sores, scaly scabs, paralysis, and gangrene.

▲
An early English book about plants shows tomatoes (left) and potatoes (right).

million in 1754 to nearly 8.2 million in 1845, not counting the 1.75 million who moved to Ireland before 1846. But between 1845 and 1849, Ireland's potato crop failed because of a plant disease. A million people may have died, and hundreds of thousands fled the country—mostly coming to the United States.

The Columbian Exchange is not a thing of the past. Like smallpox and syphilis, **AIDS** has made the jump across the oceans. In these days of air travel, diseases spread quickly from one continent to another.

People still resist new things from across the seas. Hawaiians are trying to keep snakes from entering Hawaii. Many Americans have not yet tasted the kiwi fruit that was brought from New Zealand about 20 years ago. If you look around in a large city supermarket, you will find other imported fruits, vegetables, and meats that your parents could not buy 20 years ago.

If, in the future, we explore other planets, we would be wise to keep in mind the lessons we can learn from the Columbian Exchange.

People and Terms to Know

AIDS—disease caused by strains of a virus called HIV (human immunodeficiency virus) that attacks certain white blood cells. This deadly disease is spread through exchange of body fluids.

QUESTIONS TO CONSIDER

1. Why did smallpox cause so much damage to the Native American population?

2. What in your own words is the meaning of the term "Columbian Exchange?"

3. What Old World import started the plantation system?

4. What was good and bad about the potato becoming the main food of Europe's poor people?

5. What lessons from the Columbian Exchange could we apply to the future?

"And Yet, It Does Move!"

BY JUDITH LLOYD YERO

Crystal goblets and silver bowls shone in the candlelight. Men and women, dressed in colorful velvets and brocades, dined at long tables. They talked about great art and music and the weightier subjects of philosophy and science. Ideas were argued with spirit but good humor.

One guest was known for his sharp wit and brilliant mind. **Galileo Galilei** spoke with his dinner partners about earth and the heavens. Several of the

---

People and Terms to Know

Galileo Galilei (GAL•uh•LEE•oh GAL•uh•LAY)—(1564–1642) Italian scientist and astronomer who made important scientific discoveries about motion. Galileo's experimental method became the basis for the scientific study of nature.

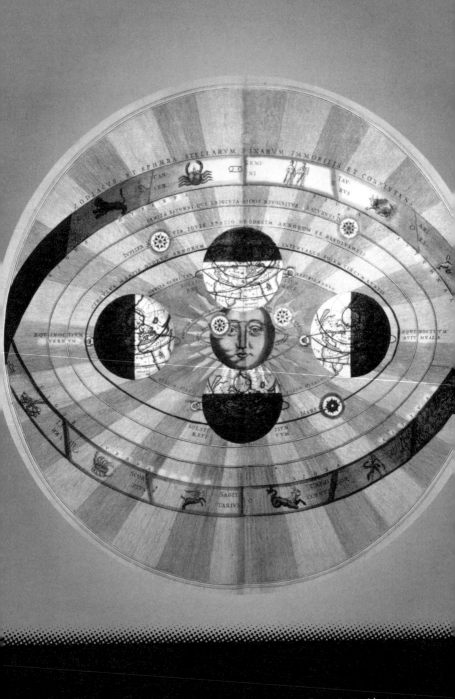

This map from 1660 shows the solar system according to Copernicus, with

women pleaded with Galileo to show them one of the experiments for which he was famous.

Galileo reached out to the centerpiece of fruit. He chose an orange with one hand and a grape with the other. Galileo asked the guests which fruit would strike the table first if he dropped them at the same time.

"Everyone knows that Aristotle could not be wrong."

A cardinal of the Church, looking bored, flicked a few crumbs from his red velvet robe. "Why, the orange, of course. **Aristotle** has told us that the heavier object will always fall faster than the lighter one." The other guests agreed.

Galileo dropped the fruits. As the orange and grape struck the table at the same time, the guests were amazed. The cardinal was shocked, but he quickly recovered. "A simple parlor trick," he pointed out. "Everyone knows that Aristotle could not be wrong."

People and Terms to Know

Aristotle (AHR•ih•STAHT•l)—(384–322 B.C.) famous Greek philosopher who studied and wrote about physics, astronomy, meteorology, plants, and animals. He described the world as made up of four elements: air, earth, fire, and water, and said that motion is part of the "nature" of matter.

Galileo, the father of the **scientific method**, found himself at war with Aristotle, a man who had lived nearly two thousand years earlier.

As a child, Galileo was a talented student. His father urged him to study medicine at the University of Pisa. Galileo was quickly bored with his courses. He questioned many of the teachings. Why must people simply take Aristotle's word for everything? Everyone praised the art and literature created by human minds. Why shouldn't people use their minds to study nature as well? Galileo argued that God had given people their senses, reason, and intelligence. Surely God would want people to use them to decide what was true.

In those days, the important writings of Aristotle and the Greek philosophers were written in Latin. Only the most educated Church scholars could read them. Those scholars told people what they should believe about nature.

People and Terms to Know

scientific method—logical procedure for gathering information about the natural world. It begins with a hypothesis, a suggested explanation. Then experiments are designed and observations are collected to test the hypothesis.

According to Aristotle, the heavens were perfect. They never changed. His **geocentric theory** said that the planets and stars were smooth **spheres** that moved in perfect circles around the earth. Earth, the home of human beings, was the center of the universe.

Aristotle did such a good job of explaining everyday observations that no one questioned his ideas for centuries. Church scholars found many ideas in the Bible that seemed to support Aristotle's explanations. When churchmen translated Aristotle's works, they saw his Greek ideas of perfection as the perfection of God's work.

A generation before Galileo's birth, a Polish astronomer named **Nicolaus Copernicus** had also studied the heavens. Copernicus argued that the planets moved around the sun rather than the earth.

People and Terms to Know

geocentric theory—earth-centered model of the universe. This theory says that the earth stands still while all heavenly bodies revolve around it. Supporters argued that if the earth moved, clouds and birds wouldn't remain overhead, and a ball thrown into the air would fall behind the person throwing it.

spheres—three-dimensional round objects such as globes or balls.

Nicolaus Copernicus (koh•PUR•nuh•kuhs)—(1473–1543) Polish astronomer. He claimed that the sun is at rest near the center of the universe, and that the earth travels around the sun once a year.

This was called the **heliocentric theory**. Copernicus was afraid of the Church and didn't publish his work until 1543, when he was dying. But people ignored his ideas, because to question Aristotle was to question the word of the Church and the Bible—heresy!

Galileo studied nature using mathematics and observation.

Galileo's path would eventually lead him to side with Copernicus. After quitting the university, Galileo studied nature using mathematics and observation. He built measuring devices, such as a scale, a clock, and a thermometer. These helped him test his ideas about how and why motion occurred.

In 1609, Galileo heard about a device built by a Dutch maker of eyeglasses. This device made objects appear much larger than they appeared to the naked eye. Galileo used his knowledge of light to build such a device—a telescope. The ruling body in Venice, Italy, praised his telescope for its important sailing, exploration, and military uses. Had Galileo stopped there, he might have lived out his life in wealth and leisure. But he had just begun.

People and Terms to Know

heliocentric theory—sun-centered model of the universe. Today we know that the sun also moves around the center of the galaxy as the planets revolve around the sun.

◀ This portrait shows Galileo around 60 years old, about a decade before he was tried by the Church for his scientific theories.

Galileo turned a more powerful telescope to the heavens. Through his telescope, Galileo saw that the moon had mountains and valleys. Small "starlets" circled Jupiter. Venus changed its shape like the moon. These things were unheard of in a universe that was supposedly perfect and unchanging.

Copernicus's work took on more importance as Galileo's discoveries added support to the sun-centered model. But now Galileo faced the charge of heresy. He had gone against the teachings of the Church.

Churchmen, who had once praised Galileo's scientific discoveries, now condemned his ideas. A devout Catholic, Galileo didn't argue that the Bible was wrong. He claimed that its words were true but that Church scholars had misunderstood their true meaning. Galileo questioned the *interpretation* of the Bible by Church scholars. If they could be wrong, what right did they have to say what people must believe about nature?

Galileo upset the Church leaders. They couldn't allow anyone to question their authority to decide the truth. People couldn't be allowed the right to view Scriptures in any way they wanted! In 1616, the Catholic Church warned Galileo not to defend the ideas of Copernicus. They said no one, particularly Galileo, could teach the heliocentric theory.

People couldn't be allowed the right to view Scriptures in any way they wanted!

Galileo backed off. He concentrated on figuring out clever experiments and equipment to study motion. Those studies further convinced him that Copernicus was correct. Galileo wrote a book in which he presented both the geocentric and heliocentric models. He thought that if he presented both sides, he couldn't be accused of teaching the heliocentric model. It was true that the book reached no conclusions about which theory was correct. However, the arguments for the geocentric theory were clearly weaker. The pope and

Church scholars saw Galileo's book as a serious challenge to them. In 1633, Galileo was called before the Inquisition.

Many blame Galileo for being called before the Inquisition. Perhaps he was too proud or believed too much in his experimental discoveries. Certainly, the way he had insulted important people over the years didn't help his cause.

The Inquisition charged Galileo with "holding as true a false doctrine . . . that the sun is immovable in the center of the world, and that the earth moves." Threatened with torture, the nearly 70-year-old Galileo promised never again to speak or write anything that might bring suspicion on him. He said, "I swear that I have always believed, I believe now, and with God's help I will in future believe all which the Holy Catholic and Apostolic Church does hold true, preach, and teach."

Legend says that as Galileo was being led out of the trial, he muttered, "And yet, it does move." How difficult it must have been for him to deny what he had seen to be true.

Until his death in 1642, Galileo remained under house arrest. His work continued even then. Ill and blind, he wrote a book that would lay the foundation for the experimental study of motion.

*   *   *

Three hundred and forty years after Galileo's death, Pope John Paul II asked theologians, historians, and scholars to investigate the Galileo matter. In 1992, the pope formally and publicly cleared Galileo of wrongdoing. He admitted that Galileo should never have been tried for heresy.

QUESTIONS TO CONSIDER

1. Why do you think Aristotle believed that heavier objects would fall faster than lighter objects?

2. Why would Galileo say that the Bible shouldn't be used as a test of science?

3. What arguments did Galileo use for studying and interpreting nature in his own way?

4. Why did the Church put Galileo on trial in the court of the Inquisition?

5. What ideas have scientists proposed in modern times that were as shocking as Galileo's statement that the earth moves?

Galileo
by Leonard Everett Fisher

Using the newly invented telescope, the Italian astronomer Galileo Galilei looked at the moon, planets, and stars. He saw things that completely changed the way in which people viewed the universe. Leonard Everett Fisher tells Galileo's story with words and pictures.

Galileo Galilei: First Physicist
by James MacLachlan

James MacLachlan gives a full account of Galileo's life and achievements and of the world in which he lived.

The Universe of Galileo and Newton
by William Bixby

William Bixby describes the careers of Galileo and the English mathematician Sir Isaac Newton and the scientific revolution created by their discoveries.

Lady Mary's Advice

BY STEPHEN FEINSTEIN

It was springtime in London in the year 1721. Usually at this time of year, gentle breezes and a softness in the air would fill people with dreams of romance. They would sigh and speak about coming down with "spring fever." After the cold, wet, dreary winter months, people enjoyed some moments in the sun. To the young, and those young at heart, it seemed that great adventures lay just around the next corner. Ships in the harbor would soon be setting sail for magical lands beyond the horizon.

Springtime in 1721, however, was different. This year, fear lurked in each corner of London. "Spring fever" had a different and terrifying meaning—a smallpox epidemic was sweeping the city.

English doctor Edward Jenner vaccinates a child

Like a great many Londoners, Lady Anne Ashcroft now lived in fear. Each day she prayed that God would spare her two children from the deadly smallpox. Many had already died in the epidemic, and the highest fatality rate seemed to be among children. In the afternoons, she watched seven-year-old William playing in the garden with his little sister, Evangeline, who had just turned four. If only there were some way to protect her beautiful children. Her dear husband, Lord Ashcroft, couldn't help her. He had died last year after his horse took a nasty fall at a fox hunt. The family physician, old Dr. Hacker, had no answers. So all she could do was pray.

One day, Lady Anne had a visitor for tea. Her old friend Countess Sofia had recently returned to London. She had been living **abroad** for the past five years. Her interest in the ruins of ancient civilizations had taken her to Italy, Greece, and Turkey. In 1717 she had lived in Constantinople, the Turkish capital.

People and Terms to Know

abroad—in a foreign country.

As they sat in the garden sipping tea, the two friends talked about old times. Countess Sofia expressed her shock and sorrow at the news of Lord Ashcroft's death. "I always looked forward to the parties at your home, to the laughter and good spirits," said the countess. "You and your husband were charming hosts. Your home was always filled with smart and amusing guests."

_____

"You've had a worried look on your face since the moment I arrived."

_____

"Yes, those were happy times, indeed," sighed Lady Anne.

"Excuse me for saying so," said Countess Sofia, "but you've had a worried look on your face since the moment I arrived. What could—"

"The smallpox," Lady Anne blurted. "Heavens, I'm so worried about the children. I feel so helpless. I don't know what to do!"

Countess Sofia said, "For once, I'm almost glad I have no children." She seemed lost in thought for a moment. Then she said, "You know, there might be a way. When I lived in Constantinople, I made the acquaintance of **Lady Mary Montagu**, the wife

---

People and Terms to Know

Lady Mary Montagu—(1689–1762) English letter writer and poet.

of the British ambassador to Turkey. She told me that the Turks have a way of protecting themselves from smallpox."

"How is that possible?" asked Lady Anne. "My doctor told me that nothing can be done."

"The Turks **inoculate** themselves with the smallpox," said the countess. "Using a needle, they open up a cut and apply a small amount of the fluid from the sores of a smallpox victim. The inoculated person usually gets a mild form of the disease and then completely recovers. From then on, he or she will not get smallpox. Lady Mary assured me that this method is perfectly safe. Lady Mary herself was stricken with smallpox in 1715 as a young woman. She was a very beautiful young woman, you know. Luckily she survived the smallpox, but her beauty was forever spoiled by it. Her face is now scarred. She was sorry she hadn't known about inoculation at the time."

"Lady Mary truly believes this method is safe?" said Lady Anne. Could this be the answer to her prayers? she wondered.

People and Terms to Know

inoculate—to infect a person or animal with killed or weakened germs or viruses. The infected individual will suffer a mild form of the disease, but the body gets the protection from further, full-strength attacks of the disease.

"Lady Mary was so impressed by what she saw that she had her six-year-old son inoculated," said the countess. "He suffered a mild form of the illness and then was fine. Why don't I introduce you to Lady Mary, and she can tell you more."

The following week, Countess Sofia brought Lady Anne to the home of Lady Mary Montagu. At the time, Lady Mary lived in Twickenham, west of London. As their carriage rumbled down the road to Twickenham, the two women sat back and enjoyed the lovely country. The countess said, "Not only is Lady Mary willing to meet with you, but she is eager to do so. She is now a firm believer in the Turkish method of smallpox inoculation. Indeed, she recently had her friend Dr. Maitland inoculate her daughter. Now both of her children are safe from smallpox." At these words, Lady Anne's spirits lifted a bit.

When the women arrived in Twickenham, Lady Mary warmly welcomed them. Over tea, Lady Mary talked about her experiences in Turkey. She said that it was just as common for people there to take a smallpox inoculation as it was for people in Europe to visit a spa for the mineral baths. She explained that ever since her return from Constantinople, she had worked hard to spread the word about the benefits of smallpox inoculation.

"I'm so afraid that my children will be stricken by the smallpox," said Lady Anne. "But what if the inoculation is dangerous?"

"Perhaps she means well, but she is wrong and her advice is worthless!"

Lady Mary said that she, too, was afraid at first. After seeing how well the treatment worked for the Turks, she overcame her fear. Now she advised Lady Anne to have her two children inoculated. She told her to speak to her doctor as soon as possible.

The very next day, Lady Anne called on Dr. Hacker. She explained that she wanted him to inoculate her children against smallpox. She said that she had spoken with Lady Mary Montagu about the treatment.

A frown came across Dr. Hacker's face as Lady Anne spoke. He shook his head. "No, definitely not!" he exclaimed. "I know all about Lady Montagu and her ideas. Perhaps she means well, but she is wrong and her advice is worthless! Your children are perfectly healthy today. If we attempt the inoculation, they could be in danger of dying from smallpox. This would be a very foolish thing to do. I refuse to go along with it."

Lady Anne tried to persuade Dr. Hacker to change his mind, but it was no use. It seemed to her that Dr. Hacker was too set in his ways. He was not willing to consider any new ideas in medicine. But Lady Anne was determined to follow Lady Montagu's advice. So she went to see Dr. Maitland. He explained why many doctors in England were against the treatment. Sometimes after being inoculated, a patient would have a severe form of smallpox instead of a mild form and would die from the disease. Also, if people were not careful, they could catch smallpox from the patient who had been inoculated. So there was a risk of spreading the disease.

Lady Anne asked, "But aren't most people who have been inoculated protected from the worst effects of smallpox?"

Dr. Maitland nodded. Then Lady Anne asked, "Would you be willing to inoculate my little Evangeline and William? I've been so worried about them." The good doctor agreed to inoculate Lady Anne's two children. He told her to first make sure that the children were well rested and in good health.

Three weeks later, Lady Anne and Countess Sofia were sipping tea in the garden. It was a sunny afternoon. Evangeline and William were happily playing among the rose bushes. The countess noticed that the worried look was gone from Lady Anne's face. Whenever Lady Anne looked at the children, her face lit up with a bright smile.

QUESTIONS TO CONSIDER

1. Why did Lady Anne live in fear in the spring of 1721?

2. How did the Turks protect themselves from smallpox?

3. What usually happened to a person after receiving a smallpox inoculation?

4. Why do you think that Lady Mary Montagu wished to spread the word about the smallpox inoculation to others?

5. How would you compare the views of Dr. Hacker and Dr. Maitland about the risks of the smallpox inoculation?

6. If you had lived in London in 1721, what would you have decided was best for your family regarding smallpox inoculation?

The Battle against Smallpox

The smallpox inoculation procedure made popular by Lady Mary Montagu saved many lives. Still, it proved to be risky. Edward Jenner (1749–1823), an English doctor, found a much safer method of inoculation. As a young man, Jenner one day heard a girl say she didn't fear smallpox because she had had cowpox. Milkmaids in the countryside believed that cowpox protected against smallpox. Jenner never forgot her words.

Years later, on May 14, 1796, Jenner inoculated eight-year-old James Phipps with material from cowpox sores on the hand of a young girl. This girl had gotten cowpox while milking a cow. Jenner inoculated Phipps again, this time with smallpox matter. Phipps and others that Jenner inoculated never got smallpox.

Jenner published his results, and other doctors carried out similar experiments. Soon the method spread throughout England and other parts of Europe. A friend of Jenner's named the process vaccination, from the Latin word *vacca*, meaning "cow."

Over the years, the battle against smallpox was waged around the world. Different forms of the vaccine drawn from cowpox continued to be the main weapon. The World Health Organization set the goal of totally wiping out smallpox. This involved finding each person who had come into contact with another who had smallpox. Each one of these people had to be vaccinated in time to prevent the spread of the infection.

In 1967, an estimated two million people died from smallpox. Ten years later, there were no reported cases. Today the smallpox virus exists only in a few laboratories. Smallpox vaccinations are no longer a standard shot for children.

Sources

The Trial of Martin Luther *by Lynnette Brent*

The narrator and his family are fictional characters; the events he describes are historically accurate. The source is *Five Leading Reformers: Lives at a Watershed of History* by Christopher Catherwood (Fearn, Scotland: Christian Focus Publications, 2000). The full text of "Martin Luther's letter to the Archbishop of Mainz, 1517" is available on the Medieval Sourcebook web site, www.fordham.edu/halsall/source/lutherltr-indulgences.html.

From Soldier to Saint *by Walter Hazen*

All persons in the story of Ignatius Loyola are real except the writer of the journal entry. An excellent source dealing with this period of history is *The Reformation* by Will Durant (New York: MJF Books by arrangement with Simon & Schuster Inc., 1957).

Cardinal Richelieu *by Barbara Littman*

Only the narrator is a fictional character. The story he tells, its people and events, is historically accurate. Sources include *Richelieu* by Louis Auchincloss (New York: the Viking Press, 1972), *Richelieu* by D. P. O'Connell (Cleveland and New York: The World Publishing Company, 1968), and *The Thirty Years' War* by C.V. Wedgwood (London: J. Cape, 1962).

The Glorious Revolution *by Judy Volem*

Nicholas Wood is a fictional character, drawn from typical court clerks of the time. Judge George Jeffreys's character and life as presented are factual. More information about him and this period in English history can be found in *The Glorious Revolution* by Clarice Swisher (New York: Lucent Books, 1996) and in *The Story of Britain* by R. J. Unstead (New York: Thomas Nelson, 1969).

Man and Society: Four Views *by Judith Lloyd Yero*

Locke, Hobbes, Montesquieu, and Rousseau were Enlightenment philosophers. The debate given here is fictional. It couldn't have happened; the men did not all live at the same time. The statements each makes are taken from their writings, but are given in modern, easy-to-understand English. The sources are *Leviathan* (1651) by Thomas Hobbes, *Two Treatises on Government* (1690) by John Locke, *The Spirit of the Laws* (1748) by Charles de Secondat, Baron de Montesquieu, and two books by Jean Jacques Rousseau, *Discourse on the Origin of Inequality among Mankind* (1754) and *The Social Contract* (1762).

Voltaire and Frederick the Great *by Marianne McComb*

The people in this story are historical figures and the events really happened. A good source is the classic work *The Age of Voltaire* by Will and Ariel Durant (New York: Simon and Schuster, 1965). Also useful is the web site: www.eserver.org/books/strachey/voltaire-and-frederick.html.

At the Salon of Madame Geoffrin *by Stephen Feinstein*

The narrator and his cousin Henri are fictional characters. The description of Paris in 1750 and of the people and activities at Madame Geoffrin's salon are historically accurate. All the other guests at her salon are historical figures. The sources are two books by Will and Ariel Durant, *The Age of Voltaire* (New York: Simon and Schuster, 1965) and *Rousseau and Revolution* (New York, Simon and Schuster, 1967).

Catherine the Great *by Carole Pope*

The narrator is a fictional character. The people and events she describes are historically accurate. A good source is *Catherine the Great* by Henri Troyat, translated by Joan Pinkham (New York: Dutton, 1980).

Thomas Jefferson *by Lynnette Brent*

The narrator is a fictional character drawn from Jefferson's school companions. Thomas Jefferson, Martha Skelton, Dr. William Small, Governor Francis Fauquier, and George Wythe are all historical figures. The events related in the story are historically accurate. Dialogue is taken from recorded episodes in Jefferson's life. A good source is *In Pursuit of Reason: The Life of Thomas Jefferson* by Cunningham E. Noble, Jr. (Baton Rouge: Louisiana State University Press, 1978).

"Let Them Eat Cake" *by Walter Hazen*

Louis XVI and Marie Antoinette are historical figures. Armand, the narrator of the story, is fictional. Anyone wishing to learn more about the French Revolution can consult Will and Ariel Durant's *Rousseau and Revolution* (New York: MJF Books of New York, by arrangement with Simon and Schuster, 1967).

Toussaint L'Ouverture *by Barbara Littman*

The characters in this story are historical figures and the events really happened. Sources include *Night of Fire: The Black Napoleon and the Battle for Haiti* by Martin Ros, translated by Karin Ford-Treep (New York: Sarpedon, 1994), *Citizen Toussaint* by Ralph Korngold (Boston: Little, Brown and Company, 1944), *An Essay on the Causes of the Revolution and Civil Wars of Hayti* by the Baron de Vastey, translated from the French (New York: Negro Universities Press, 1969), *"This Gilded African" Toussaint L'Ouverture* by Wenda Parkinson (London, New York: Quartet Books, 1978), and *The Haitian Revolution 1789–1804* by Thomas O. Ott (Knoxville: The University of Tennessee Press, 1970).

Tomatoes Are Poison and Potatoes Cause Leprosy
by Dee Masters

The people in this story are historical figures and the events told are accurate. A good source is *The Columbian Exchange: Biological and Cultural Consequences of 1492* by Alfred W. Crosby (Westport, CT: Greenwood Publishing Company, 1972).

"And Yet, It Does Move!" *by Judith Lloyd Yero*

The dinner party and guests in the opening scene are fictional. It is based on information about social events of the time and on what is known about Galileo's relationship with both church officials and lay people. Sources for quotations include Galileo's "Letter to Madame Christina of Lorraine, Grand Duchess of Tuscany, Concerning the Use of Biblical Quotations in Matters of Science" (1615) and *Galileo: Pioneer Scientist* by Stillman Drake (Toronto, Canada: University of Toronto Press, 1994).

Lady Mary's Advice *by Stephen Feinstein*

Lady Anne Ashcroft, her children, and Countess Sofia are fictional characters. Lady Anne's doctor, Dr. Hacker, is also fictional. However, Lady Mary Montagu and her friend Dr. Maitland are historical figures. Information about Lady Mary Montagu and the fight against smallpox comes from *The Life of Lady Mary Wortley Montagu* by Robert Halsband (Oxford: Clarendon Press, 1956) and *The Complete Letters of Lady Mary Wortley Montagu Vol. I: 1708–1720* (Oxford: Clarendon Press 1965).

Glossary of People and Terms to Know

abdicated—formally gave up power.

abroad—in a foreign country.

absolute monarchies—governments by kings or similar rulers who have unlimited power.

AIDS—disease caused by strains of a virus called HIV (human immunodeficiency virus) that attacks certain white blood cells. This deadly disease is spread through exchange of body fluids.

allies—partners, usually by treaty. Allies often join forces to fight a common enemy.

Aristotle (AHR•ih•STAHT•l)— (384–322 B.C.) famous Greek philosopher who studied and wrote about physics, astronomy, meteorology, plants, and animals.

Bastille (ba•STEEL)—famous prison in Paris, France. The French Revolution began July 14, 1789, when a Paris mob stormed the Bastille.

Bloody Assizes (uh•SYZ•uhs)— trials of those involved in the duke of Monmouth's rebellion in 1685. *Assizes* means "court sessions."

Boucher (boo•SHAY), **François**— (1703–1770) French painter. His elegant but somewhat artificial work was very popular in his time.

Boukman—(died 1791) Jamaican-born slave and priest of an African religion who was an important leader of the Haitian slave revolt. Self-educated, Boukman always carried a book and got the nickname "Bookman."

Calvin, John—(1509–1564) French Protestant founder of Calvinism. He studied religion and law in France and tried to start a government that was based on religious law.

Castile—Spanish kingdom that joined with the kingdom of Aragón in 1479 to form a united Spain.

Catherine II—(1729–1796) German-born princess who became known as Catherine the Great. She was married to Peter III and ruled Russia from June 1762 until her death. After Peter the Great, she is regarded as Russia's greatest ruler.

Charles V—(1500–1558) king of Spain and emperor of the Holy Roman Empire from 1519 to 1556. His empire included Belgium, the Netherlands, Austria, Spain, and the Spanish lands in the Americas. He belonged to the powerful Hapsburg family.

Columbian Exchange—transfer of plants, animals, and diseases between the Western Hemisphere and the Eastern Hemisphere that began with Columbus's first voyage.

Copernicus (koh•PUR•nuh•kuhs), **Nicolaus**—(1473–1543) Polish astronomer. He claimed that the sun is at rest near the center of the universe, and that the earth travels around the sun once a year.

Cortés (kahr•TEHZ), **Hernán** (ER•nahn)—(1485–1547) Spanish conqueror of Mexico.

"Declaration of the Rights of Man"—charter of rights and liberties adopted by the French National Assembly in 1789.

Diderot (DEE•duh•ROH)**, Denis**— (1713–1784) French writer and encyclopedist. Diderot's 28-volume *Encyclopedia* (1751–1772) was a famous work of the Enlightenment that helped to shape the reason-based thinking of the time.

Diet of Worms—(1521) famous government meeting called by the Holy Roman Emperor Charles V to decide what to do about the problem of Protestantism. It was held in Worms, Germany, where Martin Luther was found guilty of heresy.

dike—low wall built to prevent floods or to dam rivers.

Elizabeth I—(1533–1603) Protestant daughter of Henry VIII. His divorce to marry her mother, Anne Boleyn, began the Protestant Church of England. Elizabeth was queen of England from 1558 to 1603.

Enlightenment—European philosophical movement in the 1700s that emphasized the use of reason to examine accepted ideas. It encouraged many reforms and influenced the American and French Revolutions.

epidemic—rapid spread of an illness, usually affecting many people.

Estates-General—French national assembly from 1302 to 1789. It was made up of representatives from the three estates, or classes: the clergy (church officials), the nobility, and the common people. It approved laws the king made, but did not make laws itself.

excommunicated—formally expelled from membership in the Church.

fasted—ate little or nothing, often for religious reasons.

Fauquier (FAH•keer)**, Francis**— (c. 1704–1768) English administrator of the colony of Virginia who took an interest in the young Thomas Jefferson.

feudal system—social and economic system in which serfs or peasants worked the land for nobles, who in turn provided armies for the rulers.

Frederick II of Prussia— (1712–1786) third king of Prussia, who ruled from 1740 to 1786. Frederick the Great, as he was called, made Prussia the strongest military power in Europe during the 1700s.

freedom of the press—freedom of writers and newspapers to publish their ideas and views without government control.

French Revolution—political upheaval that began in France in 1789. This revolution overthrew the monarchy and brought democratic changes to France.

Galilei (GAL•uh•LAY)**, Galileo** (GAL•uh•LEE•oh)—(1564–1642) Italian scientist and astronomer who made important scientific discoveries about motion. Galileo's experimental method became the basis for the scientific study of nature.

geocentric theory—earth-centered model of the universe. This theory says that the earth stands still while all heavenly bodies revolve around it.

Geoffrin (ZHAW•fruhn), **Madame**—Marie-Thérèse Geoffrin (1699–1777), wealthy French woman who hosted gatherings known as *salons* in Paris. There important philosophers, writers, and artists gathered to share ideas.

guillotine (GEE•uh•teen)—machine that uses a heavy falling blade to execute people by chopping off their heads.

Gustavus Adolphus (guh•STAY•vuhs uh•DAHL•fuhs)—(1594–1632) king of Sweden from 1611 to 1632. He defeated the Hapsburgs in three major battles and helped break their hold on Europe.

Haiti—today, a republic in the West Indies on the island of Hispaniola. (The Dominican Republic is also on this island. The West Indies is a long chain of islands between Florida and South America.) Haiti was controlled by the Spanish from the 1500s until 1697. Then it was controlled by the French. Toussaint L'Ouverture led a slave revolt that eventually gained Haiti its independence in 1804.

Hapsburg—powerful European ruling family. At the height of their power, the Hapsburgs controlled most of Europe, including Germany and Spain and the Spanish colonies in the Americas. Almost all of the Holy Roman Emperors from 1438 on were Hapsburgs.

heliocentric theory—sun-centered model of the universe. Today we know that the sun also moves around the center of the galaxy as the planets revolve around the sun.

Helvétius (hel•VEE•shuhs), **Claude-Adrien**—(1715–1771) French philosopher and conversationalist. He was the wealthy host of a group of Enlightenment thinkers known as *Philosophes*.

Henry VIII—(1491–1547) king of England from 1509 to 1547. Henry set up the Protestant Church of England.

heretic—person accused of heresy, of believing things that go against the teachings of the Catholic Church.

Hobbes, Thomas—(1588–1679) English philosopher. He argued that a people and their government were held together by a social contract.

Holy Land—Palestine, the region where Jesus was born.

hospice—house kept by monks that offered a place of rest for travelers.

House of Burgesses—the legislature of the Virginia Colony. It was the first representative assembly in the American colonies (1619).

Huguenots (HYOO•guh•nahts)—French Protestant followers of John Calvin. Ever since the Edict of Nantes in 1598, they had had freedom of worship in France and the right to build towns and arm themselves for protection. Richelieu used a Protestant uprising as an excuse to capture their towns and take away their political rights.

indulgences—in the Roman Catholic Church, special favors to avoid punishment for sins, both on earth and after death. The Church forbade the sale of indulgences in 1562 at the Council of Trent.

inoculate—to infect a person or animal with killed or weakened germs or viruses. The infected individual will suffer a mild form of the disease, but the body gets the protection from further, full-strength attacks of the disease.

Inquisition—court established by the Roman Catholic Church to find heretics and get rid of ideas that went against the Church's teachings.

James II—(1633–1701) king of England from 1685 to 1688. James's Catholicism and the birth of his Catholic heir caused the Glorious Revolution.

Jefferson, Thomas—(1743–1826) author of the Declaration of Independence and third president of the U.S., serving from 1801 to 1809.

Jeffreys, George—(c. 1645–1689) high level minister of law in England. The court sessions held by him after a revolt against James II resulted in so many executions, they were called the "Bloody Assizes."

Leclerc (luh•KLER), **Charles**—(1772–1802) French general and brother-in-law of Napoleon, whom Napoleon appointed to lead the French invasion of Haiti after Toussaint and his followers beat the English and Spanish.

leprosy—disease of the skin, flesh, and nerves which results in sores, scaly scabs, paralysis, and gangrene.

limited monarch—ruler whose powers are restricted by law.

Locke, John—(1632–1704) English philosopher. He believed that people have a right to end a government that doesn't protect a person's rights to life, liberty, and possessions.

Louis XIII—(1601–1643) king of France from 1610 to 1643. Basically, Louis let Richelieu, and after him Mazarin, run the country.

Louis XVI—(1754–1793) king of France from 1774 to 1792. Louis was king when the French Revolution began in 1789.

Loyola, Ignatius—(1491–1556) Spanish-born founder of the Catholic religious organization known as the Society of Jesus, or Jesuits. The Jesuits were important in helping the Catholic Church reform itself.

Luther, Martin—(1483–1546) German-born leader of the Protestant Reformation. He wrote books about religion, translated the Bible, formed a system for education, and wrote songs still sung in churches today.

manioc (MAN•ee•ahk)—root crop that came from South America. It grows well in damp, hot areas.

Marie Antoinette—(1755–1793) Austrian princess who married France's King Louis XVI in 1770. She was the daughter of the Hapsburg ruler Maria Theresa, empress of Austria and queen of Hungary.

Mary I—(1516–1558) queen of England (1553–1558). She was the Catholic daughter of Henry VIII and his first wife, Catherine of Aragón, daughter of Ferdinand and Isabella of Spain.

middle class—class between the very wealthy and workers without special skills. Merchants and businessmen are part of the middle class.

monarchy—form of government headed by a king, queen, emperor, or similar ruler.

monastery (MAHN•uh•STEHR•ee)—community or building where monks live.

Montagu, Lady Mary—(1689–1762) English letter writer and poet.

Montesquieu (MAHN•tuh•skyoo), **Baron Charles de**—(1689–1755) French writer who examined different forms of government. He recommended the separation of powers, as well as checks and balances.

Montezuma (mahn•tih•ZOO•muh)—Montezuma II (1456–1520), Aztec emperor of Mexico. Montezuma controlled a vast and wealthy empire that included today's Honduras and Nicaragua.

Napoleon—(1769–1821) famous French general and conqueror who was emperor of France from 1799 until 1814, when he was exiled. He regained power for a short time during 1815, and then was exiled again.

95 theses—famous statement of beliefs published by Martin Luther.

Orlov (uhr•LOF), **Grigory** (grih•GOHR•ee)—(1734–1783) lieutenant in the palace guard who became Catherine the Great's lover, ally, and father of her third child.

page—boy who served a knight as part of his own training for knighthood.

Parliament—in England, the body of government that, with the king or queen, makes up the legislative (law making) branch. It includes the House of Lords and the House of Commons.

Peter III—(1728–1762) incompetent, brutal ruler of Russia and husband of Catherine the Great. Peter became Russia's ruler on January 5, 1762, and ruled for about six months until his death.

Peter the Great—Peter I (1672–1725), ruler of Russia from 1682 to 1725. Peter built St. Petersburg, helped bring crafts and industry to Russia, and opened Russia to influence from Western Europe.

Protestant—referring to one of the Christian churches that resulted from the Reformation, such as Lutheran, Baptist, and so on.

Reformation—the word means "restructuring or change." In the 1500s, the Protestant Reformation rejected or changed some of the teachings of the Roman Catholic Church. This resulted in the formation of new churches.

Richelieu (REESH•uh•LYOO), **Cardinal**—(1585–1642) high official in the Catholic Church and chief minister of France under King Louis XIII. He was responsible for policies that eventually broke Hapsburg control of Europe.

Robespierre (ROHBZ•peer), **Maximilien** (MAK•suh•MIHL•yuhn)—(1758–1794) extremist leader of the French Revolution who eventually was executed.

Rousseau (roo•SOH), **Jean Jacques**—(1712–1778) French philosopher. He said that people were born equal and argued that society made people unequal.

salon—regular gathering of notable people of social or intellectual distinction.

scientific method—logical procedure for gathering information about the natural world. It begins with a hypothesis, a suggested explanation. Then experiments are designed and observations are collected to test the hypothesis.

serfs—workers who could not legally leave the estate of the master they worked for.

smallpox—highly contagious, infectious disease caused by the smallpox virus. Smallpox creates sores on the skin, shedding of dead skin, and scar formation. Death was often the result.

spheres—three-dimensional round objects such as globes or balls.

Spiritual Exercises—famous book of readings, prayers, and meditations written by Ignatius Loyola.

Tenochtitlán (tay•NOCH•teet•LAHN)—Aztec capital under Montezuma, center of an advanced civilization. It covered more than five square miles with 140,000 people, an elaborate guild system, and a thriving economy.

Toussaint L'Ouverture (too•SAN loo•vehr•TYOOR)— (1743–1803) Haitian slave who became the leader of Haiti's successful attempt to gain independence from colonial rule.

Tower of London—famous prison in London.

treason—high crime against one's country. Spying and other acts of helping enemies are forms of treason.

Treaty of Westphalia—treaty that ended the Thirty Years' War in 1648. The Hapsburgs and the Holy Roman Empire were on one side, and a number of German princes backed by France, Sweden, and Denmark were on the other. The treaty weakened the Hapsburgs' hold on Europe, and France became the major power in Europe.

Versailles (vuhr•SY)—very grand royal palace just southwest of Paris.

Voltaire (vohl•TAIR)— (1694–1778) pen name of François-Marie Arouet, a French writer, historian, and philosopher.

William of Orange— (1650–1702) Protestant ruler in the Netherlands married to Mary, the daughter of England's King James II. Together they were invited by Parliament to become queen and king of England, Scotland, and Ireland. He ruled as William III from 1689 to 1702.

Williamsburg—capital of the English colony of Virginia in North America.

Wythe (wihth), **George**— (1726–1806) American lawyer and statesman who was a signer of the Declaration of Independence. He was a mentor to the young Thomas Jefferson.

Zwingli (ZWIHNG•lee), **Ulrich**—(1484–1531) Roman Catholic priest in Switzerland who believed in Martin Luther's ideas. He founded the Reformed Church.

Acknowledgements

10 Mansell Collection/TimePix.
14 © The Granger Collection.
16 Hulton Getty Picture
Collection/Tony Stone Images.
17 © The Granger Collection.
19 from top: a., b. North Wind
Picture Archives. c. Caricature by
Pier Luigi Ghezzi. d. Granger
Collection. e. Stock Montage.
21 Courtesy Library of Congress.
22 Giraudon/Art Resource, NY.
24 Biblioteque Nationale, Paris.
29 Tony Stone Images.
33, 41 North Wind Picture Archives.
45, 50, 60 © Stock Montage.
62 Tony Stone Images.
68 © The Granger Collection.
73 Corbis.
81 Corbis.

83 © Stock Montage.
93 © Photograph by Erich
Lessing/Art Resource, NY.
101 © Bettman/Corbis.
104 © SuperStock.
111 © The Granger Collection.
120 © A.K.G., Berlin/SuperStock.
126, 130 Palace of Versailles,
France/Giraudon,
Paris/SuperStock.
132 © Stock Montage.
140, 145 © Giraudon/Art
Resource, NY.
149, 156, 160 © The Granger
Collection.
165 © Scala/Art Resource, NY.
169 © The Granger Collection.
171 © Stock Montage.